A BOY AND HIS DOG

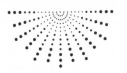

A BOY AND HIS DOG

THE ALL AMERICAN BOY SERIES

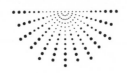

CHLOE HOLIDAY

DEDICATION

For Joanne, whose encouragement energized me, and a certain Colorado pastry chef, whose contribution shall remain unnamed.

For all the readers of taste, who support independent authors, striking a blow for variety rather than safe, cookie-cuter stories.

And for all the dogs who love us despite our flaws.

1

Last Grab

-HOPE-

*H*ope sagged into the worn green vinyl chair in the call room. *My last Orthopedics call, thank God.*

New Year's Eve, but more of the same for her: no parties or countdown to midnight kisses.

She flexed her ankles, feet aching after thirty-nine hours straight at the hospital, and sent a text to the on-call resident, Ray Browne. **Ready to check out.** She'd update him about her patients and looming test results, and then she could go home to crash. Hope pulled off her hair tie, scalp prickling from the prolonged tension, and leaned back to close her eyes for a moment.

She started when the beeper shrilled, jarring her out of oblivion. Bleary-eyed, she glanced at the display.

The ER? Dammit. Hope gritted her teeth at the late

hit—they'd paged her twelve minutes *after* her on-call shift ended at nine a.m.

Why couldn't they pay attention to the duty roster? She should have been gone by now, but Ray hadn't called yet to relieve her. Now her choice was to turn off her beeper, refusing the page that *should* have gone to him, or take the hit even though she was off.

A no-win proposition: he'd grouse if the ER told him she'd ignored the page, but if she answered, she could get sucked in for hours and hours, maybe even for another surgery.

I'm not calling. They only paged me because Ray's a jerk and they'd rather deal with me. Why should I always be the one to step up? But she already knew she would cave.

Good ol' "Hope-Will-Do-It" Hernandez.

The problem was that there was a *patient* attached to the page. Someone's grandmother, someone's son. A human, scared and in pain, banged up from a fall down the stairs. Or a parent with a kid who'd OD'd and crashed their car.

Hope sighed and reached for the phone. Maybe it would be quick—a sprain, a dislocation.

"Bexar County Emergency Department," came Cassie's chipper voice.

"It's Dr. Hernandez. I'm off call, but I just got

paged." Would that be enough to redirect them to the right doc?

No such luck. Cassie said, "Dr. McAffee has someone for you. Let me get her."

She'd done the right thing, but why did it feel like she was being a doormat? The male house staff were respected when they drew the line, but women were labeled lazy—or *bitch*—if they pushed back.

"Oh, Dr. Hernandez, thank heavens you're still here," said Kaylee McAffee, the intern from the ER. "Do you mind seeing this lady with a separated shoulder?" She gave a nervous laugh. "Sorry. It's a bit of a hot potato. We tried Ray just before nine, but he said he wasn't on yet."

If you just paid attention to the hand-off time, this wouldn't be a problem. The patient had likely been there for hours. It should have been simple to avoid that gray zone of overlapping responsibility.

But Hope had answered the call.

You touch it, you bought it. It's my patient now. She couldn't really blame Kaylee—Ray had undoubtedly chewed her up before. Besides, it wouldn't be long before Hope herself was an official ER doc, on the receiving end of arrogant surgeons or reluctant dermatologists, scared to leave the safety of their offices to even set foot in the hospital.

The little jolt of adrenaline evaporated her self-pity. *What the heck. It's just one more hit. My last Ortho call ever before graduation. What more can they do to me?*

Hope forced a cheery tone. "I'll be right down." She re-secured her hair and headed to the elevator.

A tinge of anxiety made it past the fatigue that numbed her—any day now she'd hear whether she'd been accepted for the away rotation in Bear Creek, Colorado in June. A big deal—the eight-week assignment an audition: if they liked her, she might score her dream job right out of the blocks, as an ER physician with regular hours—and in ski country.

More likely, she'd end up in an inner city somewhere, treating the Knife and Gun Club on Saturday nights. But no matter what, it'd be a do-over. A chance to be more assertive from the start, a tough doc with some boundaries, not "Hope-Will-Do-It" Hernandez.

She clicked through the e-chart of one Rhonda Sinclair on the way down. The elevator dinged and Hope squared her shoulders, pausing outside curtain number eighteen. "Ms. Sinclair?" At a muffled "come in" Hope slipped into the space. "I'm Dr. Hernandez."

A plump woman in her seventies smiled, though her eyes were strained. Her good arm held her flimsy blue gown together, still undone from an x-ray. "Hello. Happy New Year."

"Here, let me get those snaps for you." Hope

secured the gown and the lady's modesty. "Happy New Year to you, too. Looks like we both should work on our plans for next year, but right now, let's get you fixed up. Do you mind telling me what happened while I examine you?" Getting a good history was important, and a distraction from the pain would help the patient.

The lady sighed, shaking her head. "It's stupid."

Hope smiled. "Try me. I'll bet it's not even in my Top Ten."

"There's a prize?" Mrs. Sinclair laughed. "I decided Napoleon needed a bath. Start the New Year right and all." Her wry shrug turned into a grimace.

"Do you need something for pain while we talk?"

"No, I'm fine. Anyway, it's my own fault. Napoleon took exception to my timing and bolted. I slipped and fell on my shoulder. I should've waited until after his supper, the little pig."

"Napoleon's your dog?" Hope gently probed the swollen joint.

"No, my pot-bellied pig. I had no idea he could run so fast. It was may*ham*."

Hope laughed at her pun. "Sounds like he was dis*grunt*led. Let me listen to your heart and lungs for a minute, please."

THE SETTING SUN touched the San Antonio skyline a chilly orange when Hope finally trudged into her apartment and tossed her keys into the little brass bowl on the countertop. Her jaws cracked in a yawn as she pulled up her email and scanned for something from Bear Creek Medical Center.

There it was. Her pulse skipped. Acceptance, or would she be staying here in June?

She wiped her damp palms on her rumpled scrubs and clicked **Your Application**, biting her fingernail.

Dear Dr. Hernandez,

We're pleased to offer you a rotation—

Oh, thank God.

—with the Emergency Department starting June 23...

Fantastic! Her first choice, and an amazing opportunity. If she worked like a dog, she was confident her skills would secure her a permanent position. The relief dropped her guard, and fatigue rolled over her. She'd answer tomorrow when she wouldn't be as likely to make an idiotic typo.

Sleep pulled at Hope like a lover's insistent caress. She abandoned her plans to eat something and instead stepped out of her scrubs and fell into bed.

Hours later, she fumbled groggily for her beeper— alarm already? —no, her *cell*, her boyfriend's name on the screen. "Tyler?" she croaked.

"Hey, can I bring by some pizza? I know you were on call."

"Um, okay." He was trying to be thoughtful, and it'd be rude to say she'd rather just sleep. Hope shook off the mental cobwebs—why was the stoned, post-call stupor worse after she got a little bit of sleep? "I just need to shower."

How was she going to tell him she'd been selected for the Colorado rotation? Eight weeks away was no big deal, but it would hit home that she'd likely be moving somewhere else within the year. She didn't want to hurt him.

Tyler was a San Antonio native like her, his real estate career just starting to take off. He'd tried to persuade her that she'd like the town better once she was staff, but the heat and flat landscapes didn't appeal. Besides, she wanted to work where she could start anew, someplace where the staff didn't remember the times she'd been humiliated in front of the whole team in rounds, or how her senior resident had stepped in to save a patient from Hope's first ham-handed attempts at a thoracentesis, the long needle shaking in her grip too much to drain fluid from a lung.

Tyler touted the town's charms at every opportunity, but how many times could you visit the *Alamo*?

He'll be fine. We both knew this day would come. And in

truth, it was time. Though Tyler said he wanted an independent woman, he really craved someone to admire him twenty-four seven, not a professional woman who was absent half the time and exhausted the rest.

Hope sluiced the hospital smells from her skin, gradually turning down the temperature until the chilly spray made her gasp, fully awake. She changed into sweatpants and a shapeless hoodie to signal that sex was not in the cards.

The doorbell rang and she hurried to answer it.

Tyler smiled, his wavy honey-blond hair a little damp, as if he'd just arrived from the gym. "Hey. I come bearing sausage." He waggled his eyebrows up and down. "The best in San Antonio."

Hope laughed at his innuendo and stepped aside. "Can't say I'm very hungry tonight. Still fuzzy from call."

He waltzed in and put down the pizza. "Yeah? Dad says the new regs make it a cakewalk compared to his day."

Here we go again.

A prominent urologist in town, Dr. Beck thwarted plagues singlehandedly, took call for a year straight, and could operate blindfolded, with one hand tied behind his back, according to his son's tales. She'd met the man once, before she started dating Tyler, and found him to be opinionated and much taken with his own charm.

Hope sighed. "You'd think so, but since the limits are averaged over four weeks, the programs just alternate the lightweight rotations with the tough ones. So, you can still work a hundred ten hours a week for a month straight." She pulled down two plates, set them on the coffee table, and turned to get some water glasses.

Tyler clicked on the television. He flipped a couple slices of combo pizza, studded with green olives, onto his plate.

He laughed at her wrinkled nose. "What? Just pick them out." He took a big bite without waiting for her, and pushed the lid closed.

The aroma of tomato sauce and cheese made her stomach growl as she continued her point. "That's partly why I want to go into Emergency Medicine— it's shift work, so there's more of a chance to have a life." *Once I score a staff position, anyway.* She took a quick breath. "Speaking of which, I got the Colorado spot!" She smiled, willing him to understand.

Tyler blinked, then crossed his arms. "Cool. Congratulations. With your ambition, you'll be the department chair in no time."

Hope laughed and scooted in next to him. "I don't

think it works quite that fast, but I'm psyched." *He's taking it well, thank God.*

"I figured you'd get it." He shrugged. "Guess we knew it'd be goodbye eventually. Unless you expect me to follow you."

"No, of course not." She hadn't wanted that, yet his easy acceptance stung, just a little. "You'd have to start all over." *And without your dad's influence.*

"Glad you see it that way. It'd be like me asking you to quit medicine." Tyler took another mouthful of pizza.

Hope blinked. Did he just compare medicine to being a realtor?

Get a grip. Don't be such a snob. She was just cranky from fatigue. It was good that he was passionate about his job. But he *had* been a little distant since his coworker joked about him becoming "Mr. Doctor Hernandez" a few weeks ago.

Tyler started on another piece, groping again for the TV remote. He motored aimlessly through channels and pizza while she stared at him.

She hadn't wanted him to be crushed. A mature dissolution and a brave, resolute optimism was best, when they parted. Yet he acted as if it meant nothing at all.

Dread surfaced with her mother's old prediction: *"You'll never find someone, with those hours, and it's a rare man who'll marry up. They'll be intimidated."*

Every single marriage in Hope's med school class had failed. The non-medical men who'd approached her in the past usually pulled back once they found out her job. That left arrogant alpha types, mainly surgeons, and who wanted one of those?

Besides, she had no time for men, truth be told. She'd tried to make it work with Tyler, to prove her mother wrong, but ...

She was right, after all. Years of loneliness lay ahead.

Her career had to be the priority, but was she giving up more than she'd thought?

"So, I guess this is it, then," he mumbled around his third slice. "Makes sense to start seeing other people, right?"

It did, yet it ticked her off. "Sure, if you want." Had he already started? Hope forced a smile. "Not me, though—I'll be leaving soon."

Tyler shoved in the last of the crust and patted her hand. "You'll be okay. And I'll never forget you."

She almost laughed. He was comforting her, as if *she* were crushed.

Yet she had nothing but a disappointed hollow feeling, despite half a slice of pizza.

Had she really turned into someone so cold, that her main reaction was offense that he'd taken it so well? A crazy laugh bubbled up—here she'd worried so much about him. Had she become as arrogant as the surgeons she'd dissed?

Tyler frowned. "You okay?"

"I'm just gassed—a long call. Thanks for the pizza."

"No problem. Come here." He pulled her into a hug. "I'll get going so you can rest. Catch me before you leave, okay?" Tyler squeezed her again and walked out.

The door clicked behind him, but her mother's voice remained. "You'll never find someone, with those hours..."

What if it was true? What if Colorado was no different?

Maybe she'd become too cold, too focused. Her chest tightened.

Was it really too much to ask, for someone to love her? Sadness ambushed her, bringing a sudden urge to cry.

Hope shook her head. *I'm just tired.* She stacked the dirty plates on the pizza box and carried them to the sink.

Tomorrow. She'd deal with the mess tomorrow. Get her head straight, gear up for her next rotation, and keep marching toward the carrot of Bear Creek, Colorado.

Stick to her plan: secure a job with manageable hours, so she could have time for a life.

Maybe then a real relationship could be a possibility.

She'd remake herself into someone tough, with boundaries. Bulletproof, the kind of doc who could save the world.

But first things first: even superheroes needed sleep. Hope stumbled back to bed.

Smithereens
-GRANT-

*S*taff Sergeant Grant Calloway could feel the eyes on him before he even opened his own. Sure enough, Mojo's intense brown gaze fixed on him, fuzzy chin resting on the edge of the mattress, pointed sable ears pricked.

The problem with a working dog as a partner was they never wanted to sleep in during the weekend, or after a long night.

"Hey, Mojo." Grant yawned and grabbed his phone. 0601 Kosovo time—Mojo was never off by more than a minute or two, except when the clock reset twice a year.

Grant leashed up the Belgian Malinois and slipped out of the hotel in downtown Pristina, so the dog could relieve his bladder.

Might as well call my brother. He'd be up late, since it was still New Year's Eve in Tulsa.

Tony picked up as they neared the far end of the lot. "Grant?"

"Hey, Tony. Happy New Year." Music and crowd noise in the background meant he was at a party.

"Hey, Grant. It will be, if you're ready to come home for good."

No can do.

At Grant's side, Mojo hiked his leg next to a boxwood hedge.

"I decided to re-up. I'm not cut out for law, and your talents are enough to uphold the family name. Besides, somebody has to be the black sheep."

He trotted back inside with Mojo, who politely parked at his bowl, tail waving, tongue lolling, so different from the deadly stillness of his Find Sit, which indicated detection of a sought-after scent, usually Unexploded Ordnance.

UXO disposal was best without unnecessary movement which might jar a device, and if the Find was drugs or contraband, it was better that the "tell" for the handler looked innocuous to the perps. Though it was funny to see Mojo's rigid, stock-still Find Sit next to a lost glove, if Grant forgot to tell him *"Bring back."*

Tony's sigh gusted through the phone. "How long are you going to do this 'a boy and his dog' thing?

You've got nothing to prove—no need to take these risks. And women dig lawyers."

"Women dig bomb techs, too. And I love my job." How could negotiating divorces compare to defusing bombs? Every mine he detonated kept a child's limbs intact; every IED they removed kept a kid from being an orphan. And though he'd never admit it, Grant was addicted to the adrenaline, the thrill of knowing that the slightest error would spread his vaporized remains over half a mile.

He laughed. "Besides, I sweat more in a tie than in my bomb suit." Though the protective gear was hot as hell and clumsy at eighty-five pounds, a thin veneer of polite bullshit would be heavier yet.

"Aren't you pushing your luck? Seems like the odds for a Pink Mist ending are starting to stack up."

Grant scowled, unwilling to concede his big brother might be right.

Four more. I've got this. He told Tony, "I already signed on the dotted line."

Grant dug his fingers into tawny fur, waiting for the reaction. Mojo wagged.

To Tony's credit, he dropped it. "Where will you be stationed?"

"Dunno yet." An EOD tech could be sent anywhere in the world. Explosive Ordnance Disposal jobs ranged from bomb threats to WWII unexploded shells to suspected mines, the variety as endless as the cultures he'd encounter.

Where he went didn't matter—he'd have his *de facto* family—his unit and his buddy, Mojo. The dog was in his prime, with six or eight years before retirement, thank God. *That'll be a hard day, however it goes down.*

"Let me know, okay?" Tony spoke over a burst of raucous laughter, followed by drunken shouting.

"Sounds pretty wild there for a lawyer, bro. I'll hang up so you can count down. I gotta feed Mojo. Later." Grant ended the call and went to rub his partner's ears. "What do you think, boy? No stuffy desk job for us. Maybe back to the States? Or Seoul this time? You can check out some Korean tail?"

Mojo tilted his head as if in reproach.

"Yeah, that was bad. Sorry. And I know they cut off your balls, but you can still look. Besides, the chase is half the fun, right? Plus, you avoid a lot of aggravation." Testicles sometimes demanded stupid compromises.

Mojo's tail thumped in agreement as Grant poured kibble into his bowl.

Almost anywhere would be a nice change from the bare-bones Camp Bondsteel, dedicated to peacekeeping. "Yep, it's going to be awesome. 'A boy and his dog,' loose in the world. We'll take Tony's smart-ass comment and wear it like a freakin' badge."

Mojo waited, staring intently, though drool streamed from his lips.

"Go ahead," said Grant, and the K9 dived in, thrilled with the same old chow, same routine, despite four years together.

Mojo wolfed down his food and went to sit next to the door.

"You know we can't run right after you eat. Besides, we're on vacation." Grant had booked a room in Pristina to take in the New Year's celebrations for his swan song here.

The dog's ears wilted. He looked so disappointed Grant said, "We'll go later. First, I want my *rope.*"

Mojo gave a happy yelp, raced to Grant's suitcase, and dived in, tail wagging furiously. He came up with a short red-and-white striped rope, and pranced back to Grant, shaking it like a rat, before gently extending it to him.

Grant got a good hold. *"Go."*

Eighty pounds of snarling canine nearly yanked his arm off, jerking savagely at the rope, jaws clenched so tightly that Grant lifted Mojo, swinging him around. The fight for the prize degenerated into a wrestling match on the rug, Mojo's fierce growling convincing, his enthusiasm such that Grant finally collapsed, laughing.

"All done."

Mojo dropped to his belly at the command, panting, motionless except for that tail thumping the couch.

Grant lay on his back with his fingers buried in the thick caramel fur, trying to wring every bit of joy he could from the day, just like Mojo did. Grateful for the reminder to live in the moment, and for someone to talk to, someone who always had his back.

"Good boy. Let me catch my breath and we'll go out before the parade."

Mojo's head snapped up.

"Not yet. You have to *wait*. I've gotta eat, too."

The Malinois sprawled onto his side, tongue on the floor, patient.

Grant grabbed some shredded wheat, sniffed the milk in the carton, and poured. He flipped on Eurosport—biathlon today. *Women skiing with rifles.* He shook his head, watching the targets go down.

Damn, I'll miss Europe.

He'd soak in all he could before his Permanent Change of Station. An upcoming PCS was always the perfect spur to hit everything on his punch list before heading for his new assignment. First Pristina, then a trip to the Alps in two weeks.

An hour later, Grant took Mojo out again. *"Unload."* Easier to pick up after the dog here, instead of afield. After cleanup, they went inside. "No vest today, bro. We're civilians, right?"

Good to avoid advertising his partner as a military dog. Though Kosovo was the most pro-American country in the world, it was best to live quietly. In some locations, the bad guys had learned that taking out the EOD techs was a smart move.

Grant pulled on a knit cap over his short military haircut. "Just a boy and his dog, out for a walk." He tousled Mojo's ears.

Together, they slipped out into bright, cold sunshine and headed past the old clock tower to the ancient stone bridge over the River Lumbardhi, taking pictures before the landmark clogged with tourists. The river flowed silently, placid.

Grant leaned on the rail, Mojo's breath steaming in the cold air, and enjoyed the early morning stillness, dreaming of the future. His steadfast partner and the camaraderie of his unit tempered the bittersweet end of this tour and the uncertainties about the new one.

"Okay, boy, *let's go.*"

Keeping a brisk pace over the uneven cobblestones, they moseyed past the National Library, which resembled a huge chunk of pale gray Legos draped in chainmail, sprouting white geodesic dome skylights like mushrooms. Past cathedrals and mosques. "Where should we stop to watch the parade? Beneath the Bill Clinton statue, or in front of the Newborn Monument?"

Mojo turned his muzzle in the direction of the ten-foot-tall letters spelling out **NEWBORN**, which commemorated the new nation.

"Good call. That'll make for a better picture."

Hours before the New Year's parade, pedestrian traffic was picking up, and java from bistros scented the streets. Grant got a cup to warm his hands and slipped Mojo a small chunk of hot dog from the zip lock bag in his pocket.

The Malinois was reliable, a freakin' push-button rather than a dog who required much correction, but it was good to have a snack along to reward him for ignoring any food scraps he found during the parade.

The huge letters came into view, last year's graffiti now covered in a shiny new coat of silver paint. People milled around, standing and chatting in groups, and Grant and Mojo started at the **N,** trying to find a good spot, the dog's tail waving.

Mojo pulled, with a little whine, and trotted up to the dark recess under the **W.** He strained, leaning in, the leash taut as he nosed a toddler's pink backpack, tucked far beneath.

All Grant needed was for some Albanian house-wife to chew him out because his dog was snuffling her little girl's lunch.

"Hey, Mojo, easy. I'll give you another hot dog—"

Mojo sat, stock-still, eyes focused on him.

Oh, shit. His mouth dried.

All these people.

Maybe it's a false alarm.

But Grant knew his dog.

He pulled out his cell to call Captain Ayers. If she'd call in the find, it would halve the response time and free him up for crowd control. Eyes scanning the crowd for Kosovo Police, he felt horribly vulnerable with no Warlock device to jam any remote detonation signal.

Was someone watching now, ready to light them up? If it were full of C4, the blast radius would be a hundred meters, but a nerve agent's reach would be much farther.

He tried to act unconcerned, though his heart pounded as he relayed the situation to Ayers, voice low.

"Got it," she said. "Be careful."

Thank God. She'd phone it in. Get a Wheelbarrow robot here, to move the device if possible, X-ray equipment to assess Render Safe Procedures, sandbags as temporary shielding while he managed the crowd.

"Thanks, ma'am. We'll try to clear the area." He could get a start while he waited for the police. Grant bent and slipped Mojo's leash. "Mojo, *guard*."

The dog's menacing rumble made people turn and frown. A little space opened up as Mojo paced back and forth.

Grant chose a tall, no-nonsense-looking man standing nearby with his wife and daughter. A bomber wouldn't be standing there with his family.

Grant approached. "Do you speak English?" When the man nodded, Grant said, "Police are on the way, but I need your help to clear the crowd without panicking people. My dog might have detected a bomb." He pointed toward Mojo's ever-increasing empty zone.

Instead of freaking out, the man nodded again. He hugged his family and said, "Go, fast, and stay until I come home." He watched them scurry off, then faced Grant. "We need some more men."

"Yes. Calm ones. Tell them the parade's been delayed." Stampedes could be as deadly as a bomb in some ways.

Grant quickly recruited a couple of young men, a

college-age couple, and a sturdy-looking grandfather type.

They spread out to methodically push back the crowd.

Twelve meters clear. At the edge, a toddler fell, wailing.

Come on, people. Grant blotted his forehead with his sleeve.

Mojo worked his expanding perimeter, circling around both sides of the eighty-foot-long NEWBORN sculpture.

Twenty meters. Not enough.

Thirty-five meters, and sirens in the distance. No panic from the crowd.

Just a little more.

Police scurried up on foot, barking into radios, and a van screeched to a halt. Men leaped out and unloaded a robot and containment paraphernalia.

Good. Time to pull back his partner.

A shrill squeal erupted from a little boy who dashed into the empty space.

Jesus.

Mojo spun, haunches bunched, and rushed to block the child.

Grant broke into a sprint, waving his arms. "Stop!"

The boy froze in place, eyes huge, face to face with the dog.

Grant lunged, grabbing the kid. He dashed back to pass him to outstretched hands in the crowd, now forty meters from Ground Zero.

More police arrived.

They've got this now. And it could still be a false alarm.

Grant turned to see Mojo circle around the far end of the monument, keeping the zone free of people.

Grant ran into the cleared space, yelling above the sirens. "Mojo, *come!*"

The K9 sprinted around the **N** toward Grant.

Thank God.

Behind Mojo, the world erupted in flames.

An invisible hand swatted Grant backwards to the pavement. His shoulder crunched on impact.

Time froze.

"Mojo!" Ears ringing, he struggled to rise one-handed, vision blurry. Pain seared his legs and arm. A wave of dizziness hit.

Onlookers restrained him. Legs of first responders blocked his view as they rolled him onto a backboard. Someone shoved an oxygen mask at him, and he was manhandled onto a stretcher.

"Hey, wait! I have to get my dog—" A knife twisted in his shoulder when he tried to sit up.

"We'll find him." The EMTs strapped him down, rolled the gurney up to an ambulance, and slid it in.

"But my dog—"

They slammed the door.

The rest was a blur: a lurching ambulance, triage in a busy civilian ER, x-rays, and nurses cleaning the shrapnel wounds on his legs while Grant trembled and sweated, biting his knuckle to keep from crying out.

A U.S. Army doctor strode in. "I'm Major Tuttle," he said, but the rest was muffled by the ringing in Grant's ears.

"What?" It sounded like he was in a drum.

"Your captain called me in. Let's get a look at you. How you doing for pain?"

His legs felt scraped down to bone, and his shoulder throbbed. "I'm okay. What about my dog?" Dread laced his memory. Mojo had been closer to the fireball than him.

No. Surely, he's okay.

"No idea. Someone from your unit's on the way. Maybe they'll know if it's been found."

Grant clenched his jaw at the man's use of *it*.

Had Mojo been hurt? Killed?

Tuttle poked and prodded, sutured Grant up, and said, "You'll be medevac'd tomorrow to the States.

You'll need rehab for the shoulder, and surgery if that fails."

Jesus. That didn't sound good. There'd be debriefing, too. He sighed at the thought that he'd have to defend what he and Mojo had done to some clipboard-carrier, though they'd saved hundreds of lives.

After Tuttle left, the nurse came back. "You have a visitor."

Captain Ayers came in wearing civvies, her long blonde hair pulled back just like when she was on duty. "Hey."

He missed the rest of what she said. "Sorry, didn't catch that."

"You don't look too bad. I was afraid—"

"Is Mojo okay?"

Ayers sighed. "He's got leg injuries, but they think he'll be fine." She hesitated, rubbing her forehead. "You know he'll be out for a while, and they might reassign him, if..."

If they find me at fault. Or if they think I'll remind him of the explosion. Grant's hand tightened on a wad of blanket. He knew the drill, but to think of it actually happening to them ... it royally pissed him off.

She dismissed the possibility with a head shake. "Good job out there, Calloway." She grinned. "Guess some people will do anything to extend their leave. Likely, you'll end up with a medal or something."

Grant shrugged—a mistake that shot pain from his shoulder into his neck. "Thanks for calling in the cavalry."

He'd never hit on an officer, but Ayers was just his type: strong, capable, and smart. Tough as Kevlar— freakin' *savage*.

"No problem. The thing would have killed hundreds. Lucky you guys found it first."

"Lucky? Yeah." Grant snorted. But he *was* lucky— damned lucky—to still be above ground. He'd have the best medical care and so would Mojo. They'd be back in a matter of weeks: a boy and his dog, loose in the world.

3
A New Start

-HOPE-

*H*ope maneuvered her Jeep into a spot in front of her parents' house in the San Antonio suburbs. In honor of St. Patrick's Day, a virulent, sparkly green wreath glittered on the door of the otherwise august Colonial. Not the most exciting way to spend a rare non-call weekend, but it was expected, and besides, she'd be gone for good before long, probably out of state.

Hope breathed deep and knocked on the door. Music and the aroma of corned beef wafted out, a celebration of her mother's heritage. A few cousins chatted inside. *It'll be fun to catch up.*

A moment later, Nuke's nose pressed to the sidelight, the border collie's black muzzle now silvered but ears pricked and alert. He burst out when the door opened, sniffing her excitedly, his tail a blur, followed by her mother.

"Darling! So nice to see you." Her mother hugged

her hard, then pulled back to study her. "You look tired."

Big surprise there. Hope shrugged. "Just got off call."

"You always say that."

"It's always true." Hope smiled at her mother and bent to greet the dog. *Can we just not do this?*

Her father marched onto the porch, looking taller than his five eight. "Hey, *Mijita*. Glad you came."

"Your cousin Jessica's engaged now." Her mother's smile thinned, and she dropped her voice. "Apparently, she's expecting twins. It'll be nice to have some little ones around, though I'd hoped for grandchildren."

She's written me off already?

Hope refused to be provoked. She had no time to start a family now. That was the simple truth. She imagined Jessica with a little boy and a girl that looked just like her, cuddled next to her reading stories, while they giggled.

How many things would Hope end up sacrificing for her career? "That's great, Mom."

Her mother blinked, as if disappointed Hope hadn't taken the bait. "I suppose you'll want to walk with your father before dinner?"

He just looked at her, radiating the command that came naturally after years as a general officer, and

Mom sniffed. "Go on, then. I'll see you before long." She slipped into the house.

Dad grinned. "Come on, *Mijita*, before the mob catches us." He stooped to pull a lidded plastic container from beneath the bench. They strolled down the sidewalk toward the little neighborhood park.

A surge of gratitude filled Hope. Their ritual gave just a few moments' grace before her mother's inquisition and the crush of extended family. They walked in silence through the gate into the playground, past empty swings blowing gently in the breeze, and down to the small pond, its surface rippling. Ducks glided over to them, necks craned hopefully.

"You know your mother means well," he said, sighing as he opened the tub of duck chow, grabbed a handful, and passed it to her. "I'm afraid she picked up a lot of slack for me on the home front all these years."

"I get that." Hope tossed pellets to the hungry ducks. "But I won't be ready for a family for ages." She pushed back the thought that she might be thirty by the time she was finally settled. "I've got no energy for one."

And I saw what it does to a family, when one parent is absent so much. Her mother worn to a frazzle taking care of three kids while her dad was deployed for

33

months at a time. No wonder Mom thought it would be tough for Hope to find a man who'd put up with the long hours of a career woman.

"You know why we named you Hope?" he asked.

"You *hoped* I'd turn out?"

He laughed. "No, because hope is a powerful force, since it harnesses *time.* It encompasses optimism. The patience to wait for the right opportunity, and put in the work. Hope means not settling."

An upwelling of love tightened her throat, and she blinked. "Good, because I've worked too hard to cut corners now."

Her father smiled. "I couldn't agree more. And in the end, all she wants is for you to be happy."

"Yeah, as long as that means finding a good man and popping out grandkids."

"Doesn't matter. The only thing that matters is what *you* want."

"What I want is to make a difference. I'm not sure marriage is in my future for a long time, if ever." Hope braced for his reaction. "In fact, I applied to adopt a dog. A grown one, since I have no time to train a puppy." The dog in the video clip had tugged at her heart: alone and sad, ears drooping. Waiting for a new life.

Just like her.

Hope could give him that. Be the person that mattered to him.

Her dad smiled. "You won't get any argument from me. Might be a good way to have some low-key company. It's not a bad idea for a single woman, especially since you're not into firearms."

Hope sighed. He was always so eager to help her any way he could, but as she got older, the chances were few and far between, and this was *not* one of them. "Dad, the gun statistics—"

"I'm not pushing for you to carry. All I'm saying is if you're going to get a dog, get a *dog*, not some little fluffball. Something with enough size to be a deterrent."

Hope smiled at her dad, whose stature hadn't limited him in any way she could see: a scrappy bantam rooster. "Actually, I put in for a retired military dog. I figure they'd be good for protection and would come already trained."

The more she'd thought about it, the more perfect it seemed: someone to talk to, who wouldn't grouse about her long hours or housekeeping or tell her to smile more or to lose a few pounds. Someone who'd love her like she was.

She tossed the last of the feed to the ducks. "The schedule for an ER staff doc is shift work, eight or twelve hours—nothing like now—so it should work, I think." She frowned. Would the rehoming agency see it that way?

Hope shrugged and gave the empty container to her dad. "They might not take me, though, without a permanent address—I used yours for now, but if they call me, I'll have to tell them."

"Mmm. This is the outfit at Lackland?"

"Yeah, near the Air Force base. But if it doesn't happen, I'll try shelters in whatever town I end up in."

"Bear Creek, you mean." Dad grinned, his confidence infectious. He rubbed his chin. "Might not be a bad thing for you to have the company on the drive to Colorado."

"It's a still a long shot that I'll get the dog." Best not to get her hopes up.

Her father smiled. "You never know." He slung his arm around her shoulders. "Ready to face the gauntlet?"

Hope laughed and they headed toward home.

4

Thrown Out

-GRANT-

*T*hough the late-May temperature in Fort Lee, Virginia was still cool at 0700, sweat rolled down Grant's back as he strapped into the bomb suit for his test.

Right back to square one. Proving himself all over again. No unit, no dog—he hadn't even been able to say goodbye to Mojo, who probably felt abandoned, as adrift as his handler was.

No. I'm back in control again.

Grant had put in his time, worked hard to rehab his shoulder, and earlier this morning, he'd completed his medical eval—well, *his* part, anyway. Surely they'd see that he was fit for retention. A few more scars didn't matter, and so what if he sometimes heard crickets chirping twenty-four seven, even in the dead of winter?

Luckily, the Master Sergeant grader yelled to be heard through the helmet, like always. "You will carry the football through the course and deactivate the device at the end."

The "football," a deactivated artillery shell, was only seventy pounds, but slick to carry with the clumsy bomb suit gloves, and since the suit itself weighed almost ninety, the test was tough, the mock-up bombs diabolical.

The sergeant continued. "Tell me your rank, social security number, hometown, and the president."

Easy enough. Grant rattled it off. Now they'd give instructions as well as a nonsense phrase to remember.

He listened carefully to the directions for traversing the course.

"You will remember eight green fish and an orange toolbox. Do you understand the test?"

"Affirmative, Master Sergeant."

"Good luck."

Eight green fish and an orange toolbox. Grant trudged over to the pitted gray cylinder, squatted, and picked it up with no wasted movement. He held it close and chugged toward the first turn fifty meters away.

Despite the pressure of the test, he was psyched. It'd be good to get back to duty.

But without Mojo.

Grant had spent all his hours—for years—with his dog and told him everything, yet still it was a soul-crushing shock, how much he missed his buddy. To all of a sudden lose his pack, human and canine both.

He'd lost his mojo, all right. It'd be the same for his partner.

Did they pass along the package Grant sent, at least, before they moved Mojo to the K9 adoption center? It still angered him, how they'd retired his dog while he was in medical hold.

Grant felt certain that *he* could have gotten Mojo through his canine PTSD—or at least he should have been given the chance to say goodbye. By the time he found out, it was too late. Though they tried to match up retired military dogs with their handlers, it was impossible when an active-duty soldier was expected to put all his energy into a new dog.

He imagined Mojo huddled in a lonely crate in Lackland, awaiting adoption.

Godspeed, brother. I hope retirement's awesome.

Grant pushed the dog out of his mind to concentrate on navigating the course.

Seventeen sweaty minutes later, Grant knelt beside the makeshift device, to assess the best Render Safe Procedures.

Finally, he sat back, perspiration stinging his eyes, with the dummy bomb deactivated, and pawed at his helmet.

"Okay, let's hear it." The sergeant helped him remove the bulky headgear.

Grant blotted his eyes and forehead and recited his vital stats, plus "Eight green fish and an orange toolbox."

"Congratulations, Staff Sergeant. That's a pass."

Hell, yeah. At least he could PCS to Korea and join up with his unit. The world was returning to normal.

No. Never.

The new normal, anyway, the one without his best friend. Grant breathed deep to dispel the tightness in his chest.

THREE DAYS later the commander of the medical holding company called Grant in.

"Staff Sergeant, you failed your hearing test."

The cold bastard just lobbed it out without preamble. "They'll schedule another, but if you can't pass, you'll be boarded out of the service." He pushed a sheet of paper across his desk.

"What?" Incredulous, Grant scanned the sheet,

though all he saw was "FAIL" written in big black letters. "That's ate up." It was complete bullshit—he could still hear fine.

The commander raised an eyebrow at his outburst and Grant moderated his tone. "This is a joke, right, sir? That can't be true."

"Go put 'em straight, then. But if you can't pass, they'll start your medical board. Dismissed."

Jesus. Grant left, nauseated.

What would he do without his unit, without the Army? He'd always known this day would come; he just hadn't thought it would be like this, nor so soon. Bounced out after all these years, with a measly five-percent service-connected disability for hearing loss?

Then what? Go back home to Broken Arrow, Oklahoma, take the clerk position at his brother's firm in Tulsa, then enroll in pre-law coursework? He'd be near Tony, at least.

Grant tried to envision going to classes, and later wearing a business suit every day. The money would be great, but ... He sighed.

Time to make some plans, just in case.

This could be good in some ways. Be done with the bull-shit of active duty and make my own calls. And I could adopt Mojo now—well, in six weeks. That'd be the earliest he'd be out if he did fail his re-evaluation.

He imagined the reunion—Mojo would dislocate his hips, he'd wag so hard.

Being together again would be good consolation, and Grant could make sure Mojo had the best damned retirement on the planet.

Hell, yeah. A boy and his dog, loose in the world.

5
A New Love

-HOPE-

One look at the dog and Hope was lost. *Poor thing.*

"Hi, baby." She extended her knuckles, holding her breath, while the agency worker watched. No wag, but the animal sniffed her hand carefully. A pang of anxiety hit her.

What if he rejects me? Or the agency does?

Why was it suddenly so important that she adopt this one? Part of what drove her was the dog's sad story—his life destroyed by his work—and her old underlying wish to fix things.

But beneath it all, the dog represented everything she wanted: someone to love, who'd love her back and "get" her. Someone accepting. Uncomplicated. They had some common ground already—loneliness related to duty. They could help each other.

"It's okay, baby. It's only me," she said.

A tentative wag.

"Good boy," Hope crooned, kneeling, and the dog sniffed her shoulders, her hair.

"I'll let you get acquainted," said the handler. "Take him out if you want." He handed her the leash.

They'd really bent over backwards for her to expedite the adoption, almost like she was a VIP. *I guess they must really love these dogs.*

She rubbed the Malinois' dark face with both hands—a beautiful animal, with intelligent, deep brown eyes. "Want to go?"

At that word, he glanced at the door.

"You're a smart boy, huh? Come on, baby."

He paced beside her with perfect manners and no trace of a limp.

When they returned, the clerk asked, "All good? Let's finish the paperwork, then, and get you on your way."

Hope blinked. *That's it?* "Great." She ruffled the K9's fur.

Happiness spread, a warm, light feeling in her chest. How long since she'd had something to look forward to that was also low-pressure? "Let's do it."

It took almost no time to complete the adoption process, shocking compared to the bureaucracy she'd been led to believe. The dog sat beside her, impassive.

"Here's his vet records. You have a leash, or do you want to buy one?"

"I've got one." Hope took the brand-new, stiff red nylon leash from her bag and swapped it out.

"There's one more thing." The clerk hesitated, then handed her a plastic sack. "You might want to keep this until he gets to know you."

Hope peered inside and pulled out a long, Army-green wool sock, stuffed like a sausage, with a knotted end. The dog lifted his head, watching intently. "What's this?"

"It's made from his old handler's clothes. It'll smell like him. Sort of like a teddy bear for a kid going off to camp." The guy frowned. "Some people get rid of them, but—"

"I'll take it," Hope said. She gave it to the dog, who gently took it. "You can keep it, baby. Anything you need to make it easy."

She walked him to her Jeep, opened the back, and gestured to it. *"Up."* Would they have used a different command?

He launched into the back without hesitation, the sock still in his mouth.

The whole trip back, she talked to him, and each time she looked in the rearview mirror, his ears were pricked, his attention laser-focused. No attempt to rifle through the grocery bags in the back seat, though he could easily reach them.

"What a good boy you are." *Thank God he's not carsick. And he's smart.* Her worries that she'd rushed it by adopting him diminished. "You'll have time to get used to me before we drive to Colorado. It's going to be great, Baby. That's your name now."

Good to pick a different name, for a new start, the websites said. One with no bad associations.

When they arrived at her rental, she walked him to the rosebush that menaced the path. Baby obligingly lifted his leg, then heeled like a champ when she went inside. *"Sit."* Down he went so she could unclip him. *This is going to be easy—the obedience, anyway.* He was still a little aloof. That bothered her, though she couldn't expect him to fawn like a puppy. *He'll get used to me.*

"This is your bed." She showed Baby a thick rectangular pad next to the couch.

Her ringtone sounded *I Hope You Dance.*

"Hi, Mom," she began, thrilled to be able to give a grade A report, but the connection crackled and stuttered. She rubbed the dog's ears and watched him explore the perimeter of the room. "Can I call you back? I have groceries to unload."

Baby stopped and cocked his head.

Her mother's voiced pitched up. "What? You said —groceries—too low?"

"No, I said 'to unload.' I have groceries I need to *unload.*"

Across the room, Baby whined and hunched over.

Crap! "Gotta go!" Hope threw down the phone and lunged for the leash.

Too late. She took the dog outside out of principle, but he'd completed his business on the rug.

Well, crap. Hope eyed the pile ruefully when they came back inside. "A little more adjustment than I thought, huh, Baby?" Maybe she'd been a fool to put so much trust in his military training. She pointed to it and said, "No. Not inside," and his ears drooped before he picked up his sock and slunk to the far corner, where he lay with his chin resting on the thing.

Hope cleaned up the mess then called him over. "Don't worry, Baby. We'll get it ironed out. I should have stayed longer in the yard with you." She rubbed his ears, and he gave her a wag.

She needed to be studying for boards—half the day had already slipped by. Had she jumped the gun to get a dog now? Guilt edged in. It would be months before she had a staff position and decent hours. Doubts swelled: she'd be responsible for this powerful, potentially dangerous dog. What if he wouldn't take medicine, or misbehaved when she left the house?

"I'll manage," she told him. "Even without any secret K9 handshake. I'm used to barely any sleep. I'll make it work." She glanced at the clock—almost six. "Okay, time for supper, and you can learn the house rules." Baby wouldn't know she was making them up on the fly. *"Sit."*

He sank to his haunches while she dipped out dog food, the same brand he'd been eating, and stepped back.

"There you go, Baby. *Bon appetit.* Do you get it? *Bone appetit?"*

The dog just stared at her.

"Okay, it was a bad pun—sorry. Eat up, Baby."

He looked at the bowl, then back at her. Saliva dripped but he didn't move.

"What's the matter? I know it's what you ate before. Did you take me for a filet mignon mistress? I won't be a 'rich doctor' for years."

Baby cocked his head and whined, barely audible.

"Sorry, that's all you get. Go ahead."

He dashed for his bowl and plowed in.

"Whoa. Those were the magic words, huh: *go ahead?* I guess we'll learn together. Funny they didn't teach me your commands." *Wish I'd thought to ask.*

She watched him gobble his food, his tail wagging, and laughed, remembering the way Tyler started on the pizza before she even finished bringing their drinks. "And don't worry. You've already got better manners than the last guy I brought home."

6
Arrival in Bear Creek
-HOPE-

*A*fter driving since 4 a.m., Hope and Baby rolled into the little town of Bear Creek, Colorado on a sunny afternoon in late June.

Nestled in the heart of the Rockies, with snow-capped peaks rising all around, the downtown bustled with pedestrian traffic checking out quaint boutiques and restaurants, outfitters and inns.

Signs advertised the upcoming Rocky Mountain Music Festival, and it seemed like a good omen. "Ooh, look—The Whiskey Barrels are playing in two weeks!"

She stopped at a light and reached over to scratch his ears. "What do you think, Baby? It looks fun to me —not that I'll see much of it with my hours. But I promise I'll get you out as often as I can."

The GPS guided her to a white, one-story duplex

on the outskirts of town—nothing charming here, but it had a fenced yard and a dog door. Though the price was modest for the area, it was still at the top of her budget.

Hope pulled into the driveway. "They said they'd leave the key under a statue by the door."

She leashed Baby and they walked across patchy grass to the porch, where a concrete goose stood, resplendent in a stars-and-stripes apron and matching bonnet. A plastic bin next to it held worn baseball bats, tennis racquets with missing strings, and a deflated football.

Sure enough, she found the key and let them into a beige-carpeted room with a blue-and-white plaid couch, a worn oak coffee table, and a tiny L-shaped kitchen with a stained, peeling laminate countertop in fake gray granite. "Home, sweet home. Let's check out the back."

A chain-link fence in good repair surrounded a backyard barely the size of a two-car garage. Hope released Baby to explore while she toted his bed and her suitcases in from the car. The single bedroom contained a brass bed that creaked when she sat on it to text her parents. **I'm here. Going out for supplies but I'll call you later.**

Yawning, Hope let Baby in. "Do you want your bed

here under the window?" She fixed him a water bowl and checked out the kitchen—adequate for her needs.

Suddenly, fatigue hit her, from the long drive and relief that the trip had gone well. "Let's sit down for a minute, so I can make a list before I go shopping." She patted the sofa beside her.

Baby launched up next to her. His tail thumped once, but instead of snuggling in, he stared.

Hope sighed. "You want your sock?"

He leaped off the couch, dancing while she trudged over to dig it out of his bag. Baby took it from her, tail wagging, and went to lie down on his bed instead of rejoining her. He lay with his chin on it and gazed at her.

Hope suppressed a bit of irritation. *You knew he might be reserved for a while. They're trained to be one-person dogs.*

Did Baby still grieve for his soldier? Was he even alive? She frowned and googled the name from the dog's bio: **Grant Calloway, bomb technician** on her phone.

A headline popped up: **K9 Team Heroism Saves Hundreds at Kosovo Parade.** She scanned the article —both hurt in the line of duty, though they were on vacation.

"Oh, wow. That sounds ... awful. So brave of you

both." Had his handler later died of his injuries, and that's why she was able to adopt the dog?

Not just a dog. A wounded hero.

"You poor thing," she told Baby. "It's going to be okay."

He stared at her without wagging.

I just need to give it time. He'll come around. But right now, she needed to get everything lined up to start Monday at Bear Creek Medical. She picked up her pen.

She glanced again at Baby and wrote *bacon* on her list.

No harm in a little incentive.

7

Gone ?

-GRANT-

In the middle of the gym parking lot, Grant gripped the phone, shoving it tighter against his ear, as if that would change the news. *"Gone?* What do you mean, he's gone?"

A pause, then the guy replied, "I'm sorry, Staff Sergeant, but your application was denied weeks ago, because you had no permanent address."

Grant ground his teeth. He should have lied, using his brother's address, instead of waiting until his out-processing was set in stone. "Okay, but I'm settled now. Do you need the address?"

"No, what I'm saying is the dog was adopted. Weeks ago, when your application was rejected. He's gone."

Jesus. "You know that's *my dog*, right? I made that clear on my forms. There's supposed to be some consideration for that."

"I'm sorry," said the man.

"Look, there has to be something you can do. We were together *four goddamn years.*" Anxiety ratcheted up at the thought of a civilian trying to manage a high-energy military working dog. If they couldn't handle him, Mojo could be passed from person to person, his heart breaking each time, maybe to someone who'd enter him in dogfights, or even have him put down. "Can you tell me who has him? I'll buy him back."

"I'm afraid I can't do that."

"No one will ever love that dog like me. Please. There has to be a way." Grant blurted it out before he could stop himself. *Pathetic.*

Silence. Had the man hung up? Grant wiggled his pinky in his ear and listened harder.

A sigh. The man went on, almost inaudible. "I shouldn't be telling you this, but...the day before he was adopted, a general came to tour the facility. He looked at that dog, specifically."

"What the hell?" That was bullshit, some general pulling rank to interfere. Crazy, too—why would anyone do that?

"I know; it's funny, huh? The thing is, the dog didn't go to him."

Grant closed his eyes, controlling his temper. "I need a name. The general or the adopter. Both."

"Neither. I can't give you that—"

Grant took a deep breath to keep from chewing him out.

"—but yesterday we got a fax to confirm his microchip, from a vet in Bear Creek, Colorado. That's all I can tell you."

Hell, yeah. Grant cleared his throat. "Thanks, man."

Back in his car, he opened up the browser on his phone and called every veterinary office in Bear Creek. Despite his highest level of desperate charm, no one would help him, citing confidentiality. *Goddammit.*

He tossed down his phone and scrubbed his hand through his hair.

Fine. No surprise, really.

He checked out the town—a small place, but lots of tourism. Since it might take a while to track Mojo down, Grant would need employment, so he scrolled the listings. Lots of fast-food jobs but a fair number of rinky-dink security gigs—patrolling car lots, monitoring home protection networks... A good recommendation from Captain Ayers would fast-track his application, when she mentioned his record and top secret security clearance. He could handle boring— he'd do anything to get his dog back.

It'd give him time to figure out what to do with his life, too.

Grant kept scrolling.

Spotlight Security. They had a contract for big tourist events like fairs and festivals. He scanned the lineup—some high-profile names for the country music festival in July. Grant wasn't a country fan, but the concert atmosphere could still be fun, and he'd make connections with lots of people who might have seen his dog.

Works for me.

8
Rivals
-HOPE-

ope's cell phone alarm chimed, though she was already awake. Eight days into her rotation, she'd given up hope of doing anything but work. She'd hoped it would be better here, but deep down she'd known it would be this way. Her hours would only improve once she was staff, not a resident dying for a position, but there were two others in contention for the spot, working alongside her. Neither was a cutthroat, first-order gunner who'd throw her under the bus, but both were sharp and eager, so she had to stay on her toes.

Beside her, Baby stretched and thumped his tail. It wasn't that she was spoiling him, nor trying to buy his affection; she'd just decided that some of her rules were stupid—or else she was simply too tired to be consistent about them. She'd wept into his fur about the loss of a mother and child in a car accident two days ago, and in her sadness, invited him to sleep on the bed. Now every night he sat next to it, looking at her with big sad eyes, until she said, "Come on up."

"Another day to excel, huh, Baby?" Hope padded in to grab breakfast for them as he ducked outside through the dog door. Today she had the rare gift of a late start—they were doing health outreach at the festival grounds, as well as providing first responder medical support if someone had a heart attack or seizure at the Renaissance fair or muscle car show. Easy work. A chance to breathe, instead of rushing.

Hope dished up Baby's kibble, a few crumbled bacon pieces interspersed. *"Go ahead."* She poured a cup of coffee, reveling in the unimaginable luxury of a few hours off the clock. "I was tempted to go early to see the cars. But time with you won out, because you're a good boy." She ruffled the thick fur near his collar. "I'd *really* love to see The Whiskey Barrels, though."

Her phone chimed with a text from her fellow resident, Clay: **Where are you? We're about to open.**

What? Hope gaped at her phone, then texted back: **Joanna said to come at noon.**

A message from the other resident, Joanna, popped up: **Hey, the start was changed to nine.**

"Crap!" All Hope needed was to show up late—any little thing could make one candidate fall behind the others. How long had Clay and Joanna known about the change? Surely they hadn't withheld it on purpose.

On my way, she texted, and jumped up to throw on clothes.

Maybe if I hurry, I won't be the last one there.

Another Day, Another Dollar

-GRANT-

*G*rant patrolled the perimeter of the venue—a sprawling complex with grassy outdoor spaces dotted with tents for food, and all kinds of vendors. The clash of wooden swords on homemade armor was punctuated by cheers from onlookers in medieval garb. Ropes and cones separated the participants from rows and rows of American steel.

Grant snorted at the juxtaposition, and let his eye linger on the sweet lines of a blood-red '69 GT Corvette parked next to a black 1970 Chevelle SS.

An indoor exposition hall hosted public service companies and completely unrelated products hawked by businesses taking advantage of the crowds.

Four days into his security gig, he'd had no luck finding Mojo, despite plastering the town with flyers and stopping by every vet and boarding facility.

The job itself had gotten old fast. The highlights so far were Heimliching someone who choked on a funnel cake and reuniting a lost toddler with his parents.

He'd not figured it would be so hard to "be all that he could be" in the civilian world, adjusting to the casual discipline—if you could call it that—at Spotlight Security, and the attitudes of the festival-goers.

More often than not, security was a thankless job: telling people they couldn't park in the fire lane, getting in the middle of disputes between angry customers and merchants, breaking up the occasional fight, and confronting people who tried to sneak in without paying.

Discouraging to see how many people were willing to cheat just to save a few bucks. Not that it would help much—nothing here was cheap. Grant had nearly swallowed his tongue at the food prices.

A paycheck wouldn't go amiss. Technically homeless now because he couldn't score a hotel room, Grant slept in his pickup and showered each morning at the cheapest health club in town. Though his uniform kept him from going through his civilian clothes so fast, it had been designed by a moron—charcoal and *white*, for a work uniform? It screamed *mall cop* and would never look good no matter what, but it still irritated Grant that the polyester was wrinkled—he'd have never dreamed of showing up like that in the Army. And "cop" was a hell of a misnomer: the most dangerous thing Grant carried was a pocketknife—and even that would get him in trouble if his boss knew.

Grant's first day, his supervisor, Wesley Givens, had shrugged and said, *"We're here to instill confidence— no place for a cowboy. You know, just walk around and look good."* Givens had paused to spit a stream of brown liquid, pretty much the exact opposite of confidence-inducing or looking good. *"Call 911 if anything happens."*

Grant scratched his unshaven chin. He'd been prepared to lose the heavy stubble he'd grown on his trip out here, but no one seemed to care.

At a wooden stage beyond the jousters, twangy country music bled from tinny speakers, though the site was deserted. Some ballad about lost love. Grant caught a flash of blue in the grass at the base—a diaper bag?

He glanced around—no families in sight.

His stomach turned over.

No dog, no support.

Grant hesitated, eyeing the bag. *It's nothing.* No surprise, with all these people, that someone left it. *But people with kids can't go ten feet without that shit.*

Sweat broke out as he surveyed the grounds.

Nobody close. What he wouldn't give to have Mojo with him right now.

Well, hell. Better safe than sorry.

Grant keyed the walkie talkie. "Mr. Givens, there's an abandoned bag here at Stage Five."

His radio crackled. "Call it in to Lost & Found."

"Sir…is there a bomb squad in Bear Creek?"

"A bomb? What are you smoking? Are there any wires coming out of it?"

What a yahoo. But Grant didn't waste time on educating him. "No."

An exasperated sigh. "What kind of bag?"

Shit. "A diaper bag."

Givens said, "We are NOT calling in a bunch of heroes in MOPP gear and causing a panic for a diaper bag. Check it out yourself if you're so worried."

Grant's jaw tightened, but he refrained from telling the asshole that chemical protective gear, a mere barrier for the skin and lungs, was not remotely the same as a bomb suit, designed to withstand a blast. "Sir, the show's going to start in forty-five minutes. We have time to—"

"For fuck's sake, I'll do it myself." Givens terminated the connection.

Jesus. Grant looked around again, then squared his shoulders. If there was no bomb squad, someone had to check it out. Better a guy with a clue than his supervisor. Moron or not, Givens did have kids.

How the hell can a tourist town not have any preparations in place?

Grant reluctantly approached the bag, blotting his forehead with his sleeve. From the corner of his eye, he saw Givens waddle up like an angry penguin.

The man snatched the bag with a huff.

Grant flinched at the man's idiocy, handling it so roughly, but there was no explosion—well, at least, not in the way he'd feared.

"Hey!" an outraged female voice shouted. "That's mine!"

A red-faced woman in a long purple velvet getup, a sweaty toddler asleep on her shoulder, yanked the bag out of Givens' grip and marched away.

Givens rounded on him so fast his belly nearly bumped Grant's elbow.

"What the fuck, Calloway? I know you think you're some hard-ass military type, but you need to chill the hell out. If she makes a complaint to the big boss, it's your funeral." He glowered at him. "Take five, and then man the entry gates. Shouldn't be anything too scary there."

"Yes, sir." *Asshole.* Ears hot, Grant walked stiffly away, willing his jaw to unclench, faking a nonchalant chill. And now, gate duty—the worst.

Standing there beneath the loudspeakers, watching people shuffle along to hand over money to watch people hit each other with a stick while complaining about the prices. Ready to admonish them not to litter, and to stop people from sneaking in. And now he couldn't even check out the chrome.

At least he had a chance of spotting Mojo, and the people-watching could be entertaining. The women wore tank tops and short skirts to combat the heat. That was occasionally enough to raise Grant's own temperature.

Oh, here we go. Hell, yeah. A dark-eyed, curvy young thing strode up from the parking lot, bypassing the end of the line, her breasts and long dark hair bouncing with each loping step as she dug in her purse. *Nice.* Maybe he could get to know some of the locals.

Frowning, she ignored Grant and his smile as she walked past, still burrowing in her bag. The rear view was as good as her front, even though she wore jeans and a red shirt that buttoned, instead of something skimpy.

The ticket clerk held up a hand.

Pretty Girl tossed her dark hair and argued, pointing into the venue but the admissions lady didn't budge.

Folks in the line raised voices, grumbling about people who cut.

The clerk rolled her eyes and beckoned to Grant.

Great. He headed over to nip it in the bud, whatever it was. Besides, a chance to talk to a hot girl was never a bad thing.

The brunette asked the gatekeeper, "Please, can you just call back and—"

"No, I don't have time for that. There's the line, sister."

"I have to get in *now*," said the young woman. "I'm going to be late."

Late to sit by a hotrod, or to pretend to be a princess?

The clerk scowled. "You'll make everyone late, holding things up."

"You don't understand," said the woman, a trace of desperation seeping into her voice. "We're about to start."

What is it with these people? How hard is it to plan their day?

The clerk scowled. "The faster you pay, the faster you get in. There's the line, sister."

The girl cast a wide-eyed glance at the long queue. "But—"

Grant smiled to defuse her. "Sorry, I can't let you in without a ticket—"

She blinked and he continued.

"—Even pretty ladies have to pay." A little compliment never hurt.

"Excuse me?" Her eyebrows trampolined up, then straight down again as she glared at him, then shook her head. "Never mind. I just need—"

"What's the hold-up?" called a man with a bushy beard. Others grumbled in agreement.

"Ma'am, please step off to the side and we'll get this sorted out," Grant said soothingly.

She was beyond soothing. *Seething* was more like it.

"I'm expected in the medical expo! I've lost my ID," she said with a note of panic. "I'll buy a damned ticket if I have to, but I can't be late."

"Don't worry, ma'am. I'll radio back. What's your name?"

But she'd already pulled out her phone to bypass him, pissing all over Grant's meager authority as she sent a searing glance to the admissions booth. "Clay? It's Hope. I'm here but being held up at the gate by the admissions brigade and"—her eyes flicked to his name tag— "Officer Calloway. Can someone please straighten him out so I can get in?" A second later she held out her phone to him.

Straighten me out?

"Sorry, ma'am. It needs to be official channels. The medical expo, you said?"

Her eyes narrowed and she gave his wrinkled uniform a once-over.

Grant gritted his teeth, scanned the laminated telephone numbers they'd given him, and dialed the medical tent. "This is Security Officer Calloway at the front gate. Are you expecting a—" He glanced at her for a name.

"Hope Hernandez. *Doctor* Hope Hernandez."

Well, damn. He'd never had a doc like that.

She met his smile with a frown.

Great. An impatient VIP.

She folded her arms beneath her breasts, and he jerked his eyes away.

"—Dr. Hope Hernandez?" he finished.

"Yes! Send her right through, please," said the voice in his ear.

Grant donned his *everything's all fine* smile. "Ma'am, you can go right in—"

"Thanks." She pushed past him and rushed away, long legs flashing.

What is it with these people?

10
What Can Go Wrong ...

-HOPE-

*S*hit, shit, shit!

Shaking off the guard's sexy drawl, Hope ran past vintage cars toward the medical expo tent, hoping she wouldn't be the last to arrive, but of course Joanna and Clay were both there already, manning tables with stacks of flyers about sunscreen and healthy diets.

Clay gave Hope a sympathetic smile when she halted to catch her breath.

Joanna ignored her, blonde head bobbing in encouragement at the freckled guy leaning on the table.

Clay had a knot of women at his station, no doubt attracted by his wavy brown hair, blue eyes, and the straightest teeth money could buy. Clayton P. Rothrock III came from old wealth—a fourth-generation MD—yet despite that pressure, he'd been charming and helpful to Hope. He looked like a doctor on a soap opera, clean-shaven and clean cut, and her mind flashed to the guard's direct brown eyes and heavy scruff, appealing by contrast.

The gray-haired woman organizer looked up and smiled. "Dr. Hernandez? We've got you in Prenatal Care."

She hustled Hope over to a table and pulled out a metal folding chair. "Let me know if you have any questions."

Prenatal care wasn't exciting, but if it could help even one baby, it'd be worth it. This whole exercise was to show Hope was a team player, willing to volunteer.

To distract herself from the memory of the security guy, Hope glanced at the brochures: info about exercise and abstinence from alcohol and smoking.

Talk about *smoking*—that Calloway had it going on —bold brown eyes, nice broad shoulders, and a voice that would be just right murmured in her ear.

Too bad he had to open his mouth— *"Even pretty ladies have to pay."* As if she'd try to scam her way in based on looks! And the assumption that, of course, plain women had to fork over money, since they didn't have the prerequisite attractiveness to get ahead. It galled more because he thought she'd be flattered by that demeaning truth.

Hope worked damned hard and never traded on sex appeal. His attitude was just another reminder that however much she'd accomplished, she'd always be judged mainly as a potential conquest by men—and fall short, with so little time to lavish on her looks, let alone a relationship.

Still, she'd been pretty abrupt, if not rude. *No one would call it rude if Clay had done it.*

Hope sniffed and straightened her brochures. *Let's save some babies.*

Yet there were few to be saved. Maybe because it was July third, and folks were traveling? Whatever the reason, by the time three long hours passed, Hope found herself wishing for an emergency—not a real one, with true risk—just something to get away from the bored-looking people wandering past.

No such luck.

At 3:30 the organizer packed up and shooed Joanna, Clay, and Hope out.

"Want to get a pizza?" Joanna asked them, a truce between rivals.

"I'd love to, but I've got to run home and take care of Baby before my shift starts. I'm working the ER from five 'til eleven." She'd do whatever it took for Baby to have a great life. He'd already been so good for her—someone to talk to, a reason to get out instead of collapsing on the couch. The jingle of his collar, as he shook after his nap, welcomed her home after each shift.

"I'm on tonight, too," Clay said. "Perfect timing—Dr. Chen, the department chair, is the attending." He smiled as if it were a done deal, wowing the man who'd decide who got the coveted spot.

You just keep thinking that.

Hope rushed home to her dog.

Baby jumped and pranced, wagging, and her tension eased. Her missing ID lay beneath the kitchen chair.

"Let me clean up and we'll take a quick walk." She was about to jump in the shower when her cell rang.

"Dr. Hernandez? You left your stethoscope here. I dropped it at Lost & Found, so you can pick it up tomorrow."

Crap. If she couldn't even keep track of her ID and stethoscope, what other mistakes might she make? And now she was short on time.

Should she use the cheap throwaway stethoscopes they'd have in the ER? No, she needed her Littman Cardiology scope to have a chance to hear a subtle murmur, and it was important for this audition to look the part—serious and competent.

Well, so much for walking Baby. Good intentions weren't enough. He'd pay for her mistake.

Hope sighed. "I need it tonight—can I get it now?"

"Yes, if you get here soon; they close at five."

Hope's jaw tightened. That booth was halfway to the expo hall, and it was already almost 4:30. But if she took her ID, she wouldn't get grief from Officer Calloway or any other self-important guard on a power trip.

"Okay, Baby. Change of plans. We're going for a ride." Not much time together, but maybe he wouldn't feel so abandoned tonight.

She parked at the venue, flashed her ID at the gate, and breezed in, Baby a model citizen beside her. "Good boy. A quick trip to Lost & Found and we'll be out of here."

Beside her, Baby stopped. He lifted his nose and wagged, faster and faster. Yelping, he yanked the leash from her hand and tore away at a dead run.

11

Reunion

-GRANT-

*A*t 16:30, Grant trudged away from the gate for his break, rolling his tight neck.

His mouth twisted at his new nickname, "Officer DB," for diaper bag—a far cry from "Voodoo" Calloway, bestowed by his unit for his skill at Render Safe Procedures and his dog, Mojo.

Grant was starving but living in his pickup meant he couldn't really keep anything close to hand, not in this heat, so he was surviving on festival food until he could get a place to stay.

Heat radiated from the blacktop as he crossed toward the grassy area near the food vendors, trying to decide about dinner. Pizza, or another damned hot dog? Those were cheapest but if he never ate another one, it would be too soon.

But it wasn't the cuisine that irked him.

Grant could put up with the bullshit from the job,

but he was starting to worry about finding Mojo. Despite all his legwork, the flyers, and ads, he'd gotten nothing.

Nada.

Yet someone in Bear Creek had called the facility at Lackland with Mojo's microchip. Had he been hurt passing through, and he and his new owner were long gone? If this lead petered out, what then?

Grant gritted his teeth and trudged across the blacktop toward the hot dog stand.

His only warning was a happy yelp.

A familiar yelp.

Grant's heart thudded hard.

It can't be.

He barely turned in time to see a furry missile launched straight for his chest.

Mojo!

The dog knocked him on his ass, a blur of whining, yelping canine. Grant's sunglasses hit the pavement, licked off by the exuberant dog, who leapt and danced with joy.

His heart seized up, too small for the happiness that exploded in his chest.

"Mojo!" Laughing, Grant struggled to regain his feet against the onslaught, trying in vain to wrap his arms around his buddy, who jumped and pranced.

Mojo wriggled and cried.

So did Grant, tears spilling before he could stop them.

"Hey, Mojo." He swallowed and crouched, burying his face in the thick, soft ruff. "It's good to see you, boy." All the hassle, all the months alone... it was worth it for this. Together again.

The dog spun again, and the world slammed back into place: passersby had gathered to watch.

Fumbling for his sunglasses, Grant intercepted Mojo's next foray and grabbed the leash. He swiped his sleeve over his eyes, slipped on his shades, and stood.

12
Dogfight

-HOPE-

"Baby! Come!" Hope sprinted after him. Had he seen a cat?

She lost sight of him and blundered along in his wake. "My dog...did you see my dog?"

Finally, she spotted a black-tipped caramel tail waving in front of a kneeling man, **Security** across his back.

Thank God, he'd snagged Baby's leash.

Hope slowed, gasping for breath.

The man bent over the dog, arms locked around tawny fur as if to physically restrain him. Maybe he had to—Baby licked his face and neck, tail a blur.

Weird.

She rushed to her dog. "Oh, thank you!" Hope took the leash and hugged Baby as the man rose.

At the edge of her vision, the guard blotted his

face with his sleeve, then slipped on sunglasses, still holding the end of the leash.

Her cheeks heated with mortification at the thought of dog saliva all over him. "What were you thinking, Baby? You scared me to death!" Hands on either side of his muzzle, she exclaimed, "You can't run off like that!"

"Baby?" The guy cleared his throat. "You named him *Baby?*" His voice radiated incredulous scorn.

How was that his business? She swung to face him, and her retort died on her lips.

A strong jaw shadowed by heavy stubble. Mirrored shades hid his bold brown eyes but not the arrogant tilt to his head.

Crap. Of all the wannabe cops here, it had to be *him.* Would he cite her for having an uncontrolled dog? She was already going to be late. "I'm sorry, Officer Calloway. Baby's new to me, and... I was distracted."

"Baby," he repeated, voice flat.

The dog wagged at hearing his name.

Calloway's snort, accompanied by a head shake, made his opinion clear.

Hope tugged the lead. "Come on, Baby." He didn't move and she clenched the leash tighter, flustered by her dog's poor behavior and galled by a witness—

especially *this* witness. "Do we have a problem here?" she asked the guard.

Calloway barked a terse laugh. "Yeah, you could say that," he growled. "This is *my dog.*"

13
Shot Down

-GRANT-

The surge of emotion constricted Grant's throat and he blinked, glad for his sunglasses. Elation made him want to pick up Mojo and spin him around, but Pretty Girl—*Doctor Hernandez*, he corrected himself—wore an indignant frown that gave way to shock.

"What? He's *my* dog." She frowned at him suspiciously and pulled harder on the leash. "Come on, Baby."

Mojo didn't move.

Grant got a hold of himself. "Sorry, but he *is* my dog. His name's Mojo, and we were together for years."

She gasped and faltered back a step. "No..." She glanced at Mojo, who strained toward Grant, his tail wagging, tongue lolling in happiness, and her cheeks flushed.

"Yeah, this is Mojo, my bomb dog. They're supposed to give handlers priority for adoption, but they dropped the ball." Was the general her father? Her uncle? Best not to accuse her of circumventing the system.

Her eyebrows slammed together. "Sorry, but they gave him to *me*. We have to go now." She tugged again at the leash.

Shit. What was he thinking? That he'd show up and she'd just hand him the leash?

Grant smiled again. "Look, you saw how he reacted. This is *Mojo*. I can show you some pictures to prove it. Contact the agency on Monday—"

Those dark eyes narrowed again. *"Baby* is friendly to *everyone.* Sorry, but I'm the one who adopted him. Thanks for your help."

She pulled again and the tags clinked. "Come on, Baby."

"Friendly to everyone" was bullshit but Grant refrained from pointing it out.

He promptly shoved his foot into his mouth. "He doesn't want to go with you."

Her scowl might have killed a guy who didn't face down bombs. "We're done." She turned as if certain Mojo would follow.

Mojo resisted, legs braced, overgrown claws

digging into the blacktop, and Grant's heart panged to see it. *He* was the one who knew how to care for his dog. A doctor's schedule? It would kill Mojo, all those hours alone.

Shit. Grant couldn't lose this chance, and she was in the right, legally. He let go of the leash. "Wait. Please." He tried and failed to keep desperation out of his voice. "Just let me give you my number. Please, call me and we can talk."

When she remained immobile, he groveled a notch further. "Sorry if I offended you—I was just so blown away to see him again. I've been trying to track him down for *weeks.*"

Her intake of breath was long-suffering. "Fine. Put in your number." She extended her phone. "But I've got to go."

Grant punched in his digits, afraid she was just trying to get rid of him. "Thanks. Thanks so much."

He knelt to rub Mojo's ears. "Good to see you, buddy."

"Okay, bye." She tossed her head and turned away.

Mojo didn't budge. He gave an anxious whine and the woman's cheeks flamed.

For just a second, however juvenile, Grant reveled in the obvious: Mojo wanted no part of her, after seeing him again. But it wasn't smart to piss her off, and she looked so miserable that Grant wiped the smile off his face and said, *"Go on,* Mojo."

The leash slackened as the dog followed his command without hesitation.

Her lips compressed before she marched off, shoulders rigid.

Grant frowned, remembering the K9's overgrown claws. Was he getting fed right? Exercised? Heartworm meds? Grant needed to get him back, no doubt about it, and Mojo's reaction proved it, balm to his soul.

If he could only talk to her, she'd see logic. He'd show her the pictures, let her see them together. He could pay her back for her outlay, and a reward on top of that. Buy her another dog—whatever it took. How much could they have bonded in just a few weeks? Hell, Mojo didn't even want to go with her.

Grant suppressed a tiny, crazy feeling that he was being selfish, but really, he *was* best for Mojo. Grant just had to make her see it, though he'd dug himself a hole with his initial reaction. And it was nuts to feel sorry for someone who pulled strings to get Mojo in the first place.

She probably wasn't going to call him, but he'd find a way.

He had a name now—shit, what was her first

name?—and he could find out where she worked. Devise a campaign to get Mojo back.

He'd seen his dog again. That was enough for now.

Whistling, Grant resumed his rounds, his heart lighter.

Chopped Liver

-HOPE-

*H*ope hurried away with Baby, shocked and worried. Could Calloway really take him? Maybe she should give Baby back. Her eyes stung at the thought of losing him—what must it be like for the soldier?

But the agency hadn't contacted her; he'd tracked her down on his own. And there had to be a reason the Army didn't let him adopt Baby.

She replayed their encounter: showing up like that to stake a claim, instead of going through channels. Trying to guilt her into yielding her only friend. Yeah, something was definitely off.

The nerve of the man!

"And you," she reproached the dog. "That was embarrassing. What am I, chopped liver?"

The threat of losing her dog was all it took to underscore how much she'd come to love having him around.

Baby paced alongside her, but his whine pained her.

Could she not even have this? Even her dog didn't want to stay?

"I fed you *bacon*. What more do you want?"

A lump in her throat, she bent to pet him. "I get that you know him, but you were hurt alongside him, too. A change of pace is good. It's like any breakup—it just takes time, and only afterwards can you see it wasn't right."

Bottom line, the Army had refused to give him the dog—unless there truly was a mix-up?

No.

Anyone could see—any human, at least—that Calloway was entitled and arrogant. Maybe even controlling: Baby was scared to even move until the man let him. "No wonder you wouldn't eat until you heard the right command—what kind of life was that?"

Her attempt to convince herself was ludicrous— Baby clearly loved the man. But he *was* injured on Calloway's watch, and it wasn't fair for him to sweep in and take her dog. But was it the right thing for her to give him back?

No. I'm not Hope-Will-Do-It Hernandez anymore. I'm not calling him.

"The way to get over a bad relationship is to avoid

all contact with your ex," she told Baby. "I've got your back."

He stopped to look over his shoulder. Was he hoping Calloway would follow?

"Baby, *please* behave. I'll lose this job if I'm late."

The leash slackened.

Hope retrieved her stethoscope and took Baby home. "Lie down."

He whined but complied.

Feeling guilty, she gave the dog his sock. "You have this to remember him by."

Baby put paws on either side of his precious sock while she dished up his dinner. She'd eat a piece of bread on the way in.

It *was* thoughtful of Calloway, but really, how much effort did it take to send an unmated sock? Hope sniffed and patted Baby. "See you tonight," she said, and headed to the ER.

LIKE ALWAYS, the staff assumed that every woman with a pelvic infection should be assigned to the female residents, leaving the more challenging cases to Clay—he even got a big leg laceration to suture on a drunk who'd fallen down steps at a barbecue. Her best action case was a sprain related to a fight, followed by a fishhook removal.

Hope felt her chance to shine—to *learn*—slipping away, once again caught between Hope-Will-Do-It Hernandez and becoming an assertive doc who ran the risk of being labeled *difficult.*

"Excuse me," she told the attending physician, "since I've had four pelvic cases so far this shift, is it possible for me to switch gears, for the broadest learning experience?"

Dr. Chen looked at her. "Sure. Clay can take the next one—"

Clay frowned.

"—and you can have the dialysis patient who just came in with severe electrolyte derangements and new seizures."

Oh, God. A horribly complicated case.

Joanna hid a grin as she turned.

Well, I asked for a challenge. "Thanks." Hope suppressed her nervousness and went to initiate the workup.

I've got this.

Later Dr. Chen listened as Joanna smugly presented her simple suture case as if to a colleague, not a superior. He nodded at her repair of the leg laceration—she'd done a nice job, Hope had to admit.

Chen's questions for Joanna were soft pitches, too,

instead of an aggressive round of pimping her with the relentless interrogation he favored—a message to Hope, to punish her for speaking out, or was she just envious of her rival's case?

How much depth could one really go into, with a simple trauma? It wasn't Joanna's fault her patient brought both the glory of suturing as well as minimal intellectual challenge, yet she couldn't have picked an easier way to shine.

Dr. Chen frowned at Hope as she summarized her seizure patient's condition, the possible underlying reasons, and the workup.

He pimped her hard, with rapid-fire questions: "What's the differential diagnosis of hypercalcemia? What are the typical EKG and clinical findings? What emergency measures are options, and when would you use each? Contraindications to mithramycin and calcitonin? What other conditions are associated with elevated calcium?"

Hope did well at first, but eventually, the gaps in her knowledge showed up to embarrass her. A wave of nausea hit, and her vision started to tunnel, but she fought it off. Wouldn't that be great, to faint right in front of the man she wanted most to impress?

Across from her, Clay watched with an encouraging little smile.

Dr. Chen gave Hope a firm nod. "Good job," he

said, and somehow that seemed like a bigger victory than the comments he'd made on Joanna's needlework.

Joanna frowned when Chen focused on her to ask, "What's the differential diagnosis of new seizures?"

AT TEN, Chen told them, "Why don't you three go home now?"

Hope glanced at her competitors, torn between a chance to get some rest versus looking wimpy, especially if she left and they remained.

"I'll stay—" she began.

"We could use you all for another shift tomorrow night, same time. The Fourth of July will be even busier. Go on."

"Yes, sir." What a fantastic opportunity!

Jubilant at surviving Chen's interrogation, Hope drove home with the top down, singing along to country hits punctuated with the occasional pop of premature fireworks.

A loud howl reached her the second she pulled up. *Oh, God—is Baby injured?* She hurried toward the duplex but the lady next door intercepted her.

"Your dog's been howling for *three hours,*" Tiffany

snapped, hands on her hips. "I was about to call Animal Control."

Oh, no! Had he hurt himself, or—? "Let me check on him." Hope pushed past into the apartment, her neighbor on her heels.

The noise continued, deafening with the door open. Baby sat wedged in the far corner. He broke off when she approached.

"Baby!" Hope ran hands over him but he appeared uninjured, though he trembled, even his ears shaking.

Shit, his PTSD. The fireworks must have triggered it. "Oh, Baby, I'm so sorry. I forgot." She called to her neighbor, "I'm sorry. He was a bomb dog before I adopted him. I'll keep him quiet."

Tiffany gave her a grudging nod.

Hope closed the door and returned to her shaking dog, feeling like the world's most terrible pet owner. She coaxed him onto her lap, and he buried his face in her side.

"It's okay, Baby. You're safe," she soothed, but the tremors didn't cease.

Crap! Tomorrow night the fireworks would go on for hours. "Am I wrong to keep you?" Maybe she was being selfish.

Baby thumped his tail and gradually calmed.

～

THE NEXT MORNING, Hope's first shift was slow— maybe everyone was resting up for the Fourth. Between patients, Hope called kennels and every dog sitter she could find—all booked. Ask a vet for meds to calm Baby? *No. Bad plan.*

Should she phone Calloway? *No. Not yet.*

Hope sighed, eyes on the clock. Dusk would trigger more fireworks, no doubt.

At three p.m. Clay said, "I'm headed out. See you tonight?"

Hope frowned as she looked up from her phone. "I don't know. My dog freaked out last night and I can't find a sitter. I might have to skip it."

Joanna raised an eyebrow. "That's a shame. I wouldn't let man nor dog stand between me and this chance."

Clay shrugged as if certain his father and grandfather had already scheduled golf dates with the CEO of Bear Creek Medical.

Hope saw her opportunity slipping away. Invite the man who wanted to take away her dog? Baby would love that, but it could turn into a real mess if Calloway wanted visitation or to argue his case. *Crap.*

She sighed, rubbing her forehead.

Joanna smiled. "See you Monday, then."

Would she tell Chen that Hope's pet took priority?

"I'll be there tonight." Hope relished the surprise on Joanna's face.

It's not like I'm using Calloway. Not really. It would be kind to give him a little time with Baby, before she sent the man away. Would he think it was an excuse to have him over?

No, not after the way I spoke to him. Regret edged in —under different circumstances, she'd have been happy to run into a man like that.

I want this job.

Mind made up, Hope reached for her phone.

15
Grant Gets the Call

-GRANT-

*A*t the health club, Grant kept his phone close as he lifted, but Pretty Girl—*Doc*—didn't call.

It had blown his mind to find out she was a doctor, at her age. Somehow, he'd never thought about hot girls going to medical school. Probably explained how bossy she was, though. *That's pretty sexist, Calloway.*

Still, he kept remembering her breathless speech. It was only a short leap to fantasizing about her asking him to undress, pressing a stethoscope to his chest as she listened, those lips parted, before she glided her hands along his skin, one up and one down...

He shook himself and went into the locker room.

He'd have to visit a laundromat next—he'd be changing into his last clean clothes after he showered.

His phone rang and he lunged for it. An out-of-state area code—could it be her? "Hello."

"Mr. Calloway? This is Hope Hernandez. Baby's owner." She sounded reluctant—but she'd called.

Hope! That's right. "Hey, Doc. Good to hear from you." Grant held his breath.

"Yeah, about that..." She sighed. "I'm worried how he'll do with the fireworks, but I have to work and can't find a sitter." A pause. "I'm sorry to bother you at the last minute, but do you think—"

"No problem." *Yes!* However grudging, her request meant she cared more about the dog than her pride.

This was perfect—it gave him a chance to get his foot in the door. "When do you need me? I was about to shower and do some laundry."

Desperation lay beneath her words. "I have to be in the ER by six. You're welcome to do both here." She gave him her address.

"I'll be there by five."

Whistling, he shoved dirty clothes into a bag and cleaned out his truck, so it didn't look lived-in. What she didn't know wouldn't hurt her.

He stopped at a grocery store on the way to buy some hot dogs for Mojo. It wasn't a bribe, nor cheating—just a reminder, for training—she'd probably let Mojo's manners go.

Anything Grant could do to show Mojo was better

off with him would be worthwhile. He put some clippers into the basket so he could trim the dog's nails.

Grant pulled up in front of a modest duplex with scraggly grass in the front yard. He pushed the hot dogs deeper into his backpack and knocked on the door.

It jerked open and Pretty Girl peered out, wearing blue scrubs. Her hair was pulled back but dark tendrils escaped to frame her gorgeous brown eyes.

Why had he never had a medical fantasy up to now?

"Hey," he said.

"Hi. Thanks for coming." She gripped the doorframe. "I appreciate your watching him—"

"No problem." Was she going to let him in? "I'm happy to come any time, for anything you need." Shit, maybe not the best word choice. He smiled to distract her from the unintentional double entendre.

Her eyes dropped to his lips, then narrowed. "I don't need anything from you, just..." Her face flushed and she tossed her head. "Look, this is only about Baby, okay? A one-time thing, for his sake, *not* a chance to ... to..." She bit her lip, cheeks flaming.

Grant laughed. "Get *acquainted?*"

She rolled her eyes. "Right. Don't even think about it."

Too late for that.

Grant grinned. "Wouldn't dream of it." Too late for that, too—he'd awakened this morning with her taste fading from his tongue.

But what she didn't know wouldn't hurt her, and one more thing she didn't know was that Grant couldn't resist a challenge.

He sauntered inside when she wordlessly held open the door.

Mojo freakin' lost it, whirling in joy when Grant entered, while Hope looked on with a sour expression.

Pumped to see Mojo again, Grant ruffled the dog's fur, resisting the temptation to drop to his knees to embrace him.

Grant lifted his head to take in the room—a puke-beige carpet, bookshelves, a tiny kitchen. Coffee table piled high with magazines, the sock he'd sent Mojo underneath.

His respect for her ticked up a notch. She cared more about the dog than a perfect house.

"The shower's through there. You can sleep on the couch if you want, until I get back." She gestured to a pile of sheets and blankets. "It's a little lumpy, but not bad."

"It'll be great."

Grant picked up Mojo's front paw, frowning. "I'll

trim his nails while I'm here. It's bad for his feet to let them get so long." *Geez, just stop talking.*

Sure enough, her lips compressed.

Grant gave her his best smile. "Want to see some pictures of us? Some real 'Baby' pictures?" If she could see their history, how could she not understand?

She sniffed, as if she could tell what he was up to. "I've got to get going, so let me show you where things are."

Grant noted with approval that she had the same kibble Mojo liked. Next to the couch was a red corduroy dog bed, barely used. Had she got it just because he was coming over? "So, any medicines?" He watched for her reaction.

"No, his heartworm combo isn't until the fifteenth."

Okay, good. She's on top of that, at least.

Grant squashed the image of her on top of him, her hair slipping down over her shoulders to spill over her breasts.

Down, son. You're here for your dog.

He followed her to the kitchen, Mojo like his shadow.

"Cook if you want, though I don't have much here." Her eyes swept past him to the door. "I need to grab the mail."

Hope slipped outside and came in with a sheaf of flyers.

Yesterday's mail, since today was a holiday.

Not a good sign. "What time do you feed him?" he asked. "I want to be sure to keep to the same schedule."

It was probably all over the place, but would she admit it?

Hope tossed her head and ripped open an envelope instead of answering, and Grant grinned at Mojo.

I've got this, buddy.

Silence.

Grant looked up.

She stared at a letter in her hands, her face pale.

"Doc? You okay?"

She blinked and smiled, fake as hell. "I'm fine. Feed him at six. See you later."

She pushed the letter under a pile of pizza flyers, swept up her bag, and the door closed behind her.

Huh.

He dismissed her reaction, thrilled to spend time with Mojo. "Looks like it's you and me again, huh, boy?" Grant waited for the sound of her Jeep to fade, then sat on the floor with Mojo between his legs, almost like a lapdog.

"I'm so glad to see you again, buddy," he whispered, as the dog wriggled happily, tail thumping.

The fullness in Grant's throat eased after a few minutes, and he sent Mojo out back. While the dog marked the perimeter, Grant dragged his hand over the rope toy in his bag to gather the scent and tucked it behind a shelved book.

"Mojo, *come.*" He held out his empty palm for the dog to sniff. *"Find."*

The dog yelped with joy and raced around the room, snuffling and wagging hard. Backtracking, he sniffed the bookcase and plunked down next to it, his stare intense.

"Good boy." Grant pulled out the rope for a brisk tug-of-war, happy that Mojo seemed as strong as ever.

"Okay," he said after ten minutes. *"All done.* Let's trim those nails, then we'll file 'em down with a walk before dinner."

He carefully tended to his buddy. "Damn, I missed you."

Grant put away the clippers. *"Let's go."*

They explored the neighborhood, the crisp mountain air cool compared to Tulsa, and Grant's world felt right again.

After they got back from the walk he peeked in the fridge.

Not much there. A few tubs of yogurt, leftover Chinese takeout … *bacon?* "Weird for a doc to be eating that," he told the dog. "I should have stopped for something."

Grant opened the freezer—a stack of frozen pot pies, all turkey. "Geez. We've got to get you out of here, Mojo. Even I can do better than that."

He grabbed one—he'd replace it later—and set the little frozen brick on the countertop. "*Leave it.*"

He strode in to take a quick rinse while the oven preheated. After dinner, he'd do a load of laundry, including the towel he used.

A weird burnt food smell penetrated the scent of shampoo. A second later, the smoke alarm went off, and so did Mojo, barking loudly.

Shit!

Grant stumbled out of the shower, wrapped a towel around his waist, and dashed into the kitchen. Smoke leaked from the oven while Mojo barked and whined.

"Mojo, *all done.* It's okay."

The dog ceased and slunk to a far corner.

Grant switched on the vent fan, an idiotic device that simply jetted the smoke straight up to the smoke detector. He madly fanned the alarm with a kitchen towel.

The shrill assault stopped, but someone was banging on the front door like a storm trooper.

Great. He strode over and yanked it open.

A blonde in her thirties snapped, "Look, I've had it with—oh." She blinked. "Well, *hello*," she cooed. "Hope didn't tell me she had company. I'm Tiffany, from next door." She looked him up and down. "Need a hand with anything?"

"No, ma'am, I'm good."

She gave him a sultry smile. "I guess so. Let me know if you need some sugar or anything else." She sashayed back to her half of the duplex.

"Not happening," he muttered, and shut the door. "What the hell was that, though?"

He opened a couple of windows and cautiously looked inside the oven. Smoke rolled out from—*dirty dishes?*

Grant flapped the dishtowel to disperse the cloud. "Geez, is she that much of a slob, Mojo? Cleaned house by shoving things in here?" But that wasn't fair—Grant knew how it could be with a long on-call stretch.

He left the oven door open to cool and gazed around with new eyes. The bathroom had been clean, and the kitchen okay, but the carpet needed vacuuming, and the coffee table was cluttered six inches deep with medical journals.

"This is *not* a woman who has time for a dog, buddy."

He read the names of the articles.

"FDA Grants Accelerated Approval to Dostar-limab-gxly for dMMR Endometrial Cancer" and

"Enfortumab Vedotin-ejfv After PD-1 or PD-L1 Inhibitor Therapy for Cisplatin-Ineligible Patients With Advanced Urothelial Carcinoma."

Grant raised an eyebrow at Mojo. "What the hell does that even *mean,* other than she must be smart? You think if I went into law, it'd impress a woman like that?"

Mojo just grinned at him.

"Me, neither. Guess it's pizza tonight, huh?" Grant scooped up the sheaf of pizza flyers and the bottom sheet fell out.

A single page, the message spelled out in letters cut from magazines:

I'M WATCHING YOU.

Jesus. What the hell? His eyes involuntarily flicked to the windows. "She's got a stalker, Mojo? Damn. Maybe she needs you more than I do."

Grant glanced at the letter again and shook his head. *Creepy.* Devious, though, with no direct threat.

What could he do to help? She hadn't said a thing —shit, did she think it was him?

Nah, she wouldn't have left me here with Mojo.

There had to be something he could do.

Grant cleaned the mess from the oven while he mulled things over.

Maybe I'll call Tony.

16
A Sick Joke?

-HOPE-

*H*ope borrowed a baseball bat from the bin on the porch, stashing it behind the front seat—she'd put one in the umbrella stand later. She drove in to work, nauseated, **"I'M WATCHING YOU"** looping in her mind.

The first letter had said, **"WELCOME TO BEAR CREEK."**

She'd dismissed it as a quirky greeting from neighborhood kids too young to realize the cut-and-paste would invoke stalker movies, and because it had been shoved into her box instead of postmarked.

It had to be a sick joke. Who'd want to harm her? Yet it was addressed to Dr. Hernandez.

Her mind flashed to the patients she'd seen. The drug-seeking woman who'd wanted a bunch of oxy? Someone who'd developed a weird crush on her during the hours they sat in the ER, watching her go back and forth, then followed her home? Some guy at a gas station or the grocery store? The festival, even?

Crap—was it a staff member? That would explain how they got her address.

Suddenly, she felt horribly vulnerable. *Thank God for Baby.* She'd felt guilty, seeing Grant with him, but no way would she part with her dog now.

Could it be Grant? Just for a second, doubt crept in before utter certainty blasted it to bits.

No. There's no way it's Grant. He'd had a military secret security clearance, and also had been vetted for Spotlight. More importantly, he was a man who loved his dog, and Baby loved him. That counted for more in her book than any denials. Besides, the first letter had arrived before he'd reunited with Baby. His goal seemed to be her dog, nothing more.

On arrival to the ER, Hope checked in with the attending, and soon Clay strolled in behind Joanna.

The attending physician assigned their patients. It helped to be busy, but Hope found herself eyeing the employees, patients, and families.

It's got to be a joke.

During a lull, the trio of residents trooped down to the physician's lounge for coffee. Hope watched them for clues they wished her ill. Surely, neither would stoop to such tactics.

"Look at this." Clay spun a glossy flyer onto the table with a smirk. "Guess you two could find work there."

Geez. Hope glanced at it—a place called AlphaMed, recruiting for docs to fill short-term vacancies—and sipped her coffee instead of rolling her eyes.

"You seem distracted," Joanna told Hope.

"Have you guys... seen anyone acting strangely? Or asking about me?"

Clay smiled. "About you? Sure. I overheard some x-ray techs talk about both of you. Wishful thinking stuff. Why?"

Crap—*was* it a staff member?

"I got a weird letter," Hope said.

"Oh?" Clay raised an eyebrow. "Like what?"

"Anonymous. Said they were watching me."

Clay's other eyebrow lifted in surprise.

Joanna tilted her head and stared at Hope like she was doing a psych evaluation on someone claiming to be the Queen of England. "That's... disturbing. What are you going to do?"

Neither resident gave any hint of nervousness. *Surely it's not them.*

"Do?" Hope smiled with all the bravado she could muster. "Probably nothing. There was no threat, and it's not illegal to send anonymous letters."

How many people worked at Bear Creek Medical?

I'll ask Mrs. Phelps for an appointment. The residency coordinator could check to see if someone had accessed Hope's personnel records.

All three beepers went off at once.

Hope grinned. "They're playing our song." She pushed back her chair.

The ER was hopping when they got back, and adrenaline recharged her. As eleven p.m. rolled around, the wait times remained high, with new folks still coming in.

"Can you stay longer?" Chen asked.

The three locked eyes in silent challenge. "Yes," they said in unison.

Hope stepped off to the side and called Grant. "Everything okay?"

"Sure thing, Doc." His smile came through the line.

"They still need me here. I don't know for how long." She braced herself for a snarky reply. "Can you please—"

"Got it covered," he said.

Wow, he'd skipped the chance to needle her about her schedule. Maybe because there was no need to say it?

She stepped on her guilt. Not enough of her to go around. As usual. When would she finally get used to it?

HOURS LATER, Hope clipped off her last suture, admiring her work: seventeen interrupted stitches along the man's medial shoulder blade.

"Keep it clean and dry," she told him as she bandaged the wound. "You're sure you can't tell me more about what happened, Mr. Larkin?"

"Like I said, I just tripped and fell on my knife."

Right. Hope didn't push it. "Well, be careful out there."

It was nearly two when she arrived home. He'd left the porch light on for her. *Thoughtful.*

When she entered, Grant sat up on the couch, blinking, his sleep-tousled hair sexy. He wore shorts and a T-shirt that said, **EOD: It's a Blast!** clung to his muscular torso.

Beside him, Baby wagged.

"Hey, Pretty Girl."

Who did he think he was, calling her that? But that husky voice made her shiver, and Hope swallowed her retort—the man was half-asleep, and he'd done her such a favor. "How'd Baby do?"

"Mojo did okay." Grant rubbed his eyes. "Want something to eat? I've got pizza in the fridge."

"Thanks." She glanced at the dish rack—full of

clean plates and pans. How could he have used so—*oh, crap.*

Her face warmed. "Looks like you washed up."

"Yeah. Had a smoke alarm incident. I'm afraid I melted one of your plastic bowls."

Hope giggled—she'd passed into that stage of fatigue where everything threatened to either make her laugh or cry. "I ran out of time, and it's been so busy..." She stopped, too tired to justify herself to him.

"I get it," he said softly. "I had long hours sometimes, too. I'd better get out of here so you can sleep."

"No, wait," she blurted out, stumbling at the realization that he was the only one she *could* trust. "Stay —if you want to, I mean. Since it's so late." Her cheeks heated anew.

His slow smile revealed a dimple. "I can't refuse a request like that."

"You're still sleeping on the couch. Come on, Baby."

Grant put his hand over his heart in mock dismay. "What? He sleeps with you? On the bed?"

"He's a good boy." Hope patted Baby, who grinned at Grant.

"Damn." He shook his head. "That's one lucky dog." He yawned and stretched. "I'm off work tomorrow. What time do you need to be up? I'll tend to Mojo if you want to sleep in."

Ooh. He couldn't have offered her anything better —well, anything she might actually accept. "I have a meeting with the hospital administration, so I need to be up by ten. I'll grab groceries after that, before my shift." Three extra hours of sleep, if he'd take care of her dog—an unbelievable luxury. "Thanks."

"No problem." Grant rubbed Baby's ears and stretched out on the couch again, biceps bunched, fingers laced behind his head.

The broad expanse of chest called to her, urging her to lie down next to him, trusting in his strength to keep her safe.

Damn. That stupid letter had her all shook up.

She turned away from temptation, but his voice followed her into the bedroom.

"Goodnight, Doc."

WHEN SHE AWOKE the next morning, they were gone. Grant had left a note: **Out exploring.** His truck was parked outside, so he hadn't absconded with Baby.

Guilt tugged at her for even thinking that. It was nice of him to stay and free her up to concentrate on the meeting she'd requested with Mrs. Phelps, the resident coordinator.

Still, Hope couldn't avoid a twinge of jealousy— here she was in this gorgeous part of the country, with one of the best country music events nation- wide, and she might as well be living in Antarctica, for all the time she got to spend outside the hospital.

Stop whining. You're building your future. Hope shook it off and drove in for her meeting.

To her surprise, the hospital CEO, Raymond Koonce, sat next to Mrs. Phelps.

Crap. This was *not* the kind of attention Hope wanted. Why had Phelps called him in?

"Raymond likes to be involved in all aspects of hospital relations," said the coordinator, with a nervous glance at the older man.

"What can I do for you, Dr. Hernandez?" Koonce smiled at Hope, his eyes kind behind old-school black plastic frames.

"I'm hoping for advice," she began. "I received an anonymous letter that said they were watching me. I know it could be anyone, but is it possible for the IT department to see if anyone here accessed my personnel files for my address?"

He raised his eyebrows. "You think it's someone on staff?"

"I... just thought I'd check here first instead of

going to the police, though there might be finger-
prints on the letter."

"Good call." Koonce frowned. "We've worked hard
to develop a stellar program, and rumors of stalkers
associated with the hospital would be anathema. I
can't overestimate the importance of discretion,
rather than a premature decision to disseminate this
to law enforcement—or your colleagues."

Disappointing, but he was right that the gossip
would slowly percolate out.

Koonce shook his head. "We'll do a thorough
investigation on who had access to your information."

He gave her a genial smile. "I'm told you're doing a
superb job so far in the ER and are interested in relo-
cating here. Certainly, your safety is paramount, but
I'm sure you understand that personnel employed by
Bear Creek Medical don't draw any attention to our
facilities, beyond our excellent patient care."

Wow. That's subtle. "I understand. Thank you for
your help." Hope smiled and shook his hand, discouraged that the facility's reputation trumped her peace
of mind. *At least they'll look into it.*

She stopped for a few groceries and drove home,
the snowy peaks shining in the distance.

Grant's laugh came through the screen door,
talking to Baby like an old friend.

I guess he is. Hope sighed, grabbed the bags, and

walked inside, past the mail jammed into the box on the porch.

Baby pranced up to her and she bent to pat him. "Hey, guys."

"Hey, Pretty Girl." Grant smiled at her narrowed eyes.

Baby pirouetted.

"Oh, you want a snack?" Hope put down her bags, opened the fridge and took a piece of crisp bacon from a zip lock. "Here you go, Baby."

Grant's eyebrows rose. "You're feeding him *bacon?*" His belly growled.

"Sure. Did you want some?"

Baby licked his lips and wagged, but Grant frowned and crossed his arms. "No. It's bad for him to have too much junk food."

"I suppose." She unpacked the bag. "I guess it's okay that you eat even worse than Baby? Speaking of which, I picked up some buns to go with the hot dogs you brought."

Grant's face went still, then he barked a laugh. "Anything more to bring in?"

Only the mail.

Dread washed through her, and she paused with eggs and coffee in her hands. "No, but could you grab the mail?" If there was another letter, it would be a relief to tell someone. Besides, Grant might have some ideas.

"Sure." He stepped out onto the porch and returned with a folded wad of mail. He tossed it onto the countertop.

A white envelope with familiar block letters slid out from the rest, labeled **DR. HERNANDEZ.**

77

Mojo Shows his Stuff

-GRANT-

*B*lood drained from Hope's face, and she clutched the countertop.

Frowning, Grant glanced at the long envelope. *Shit, is it another letter?* "What's wrong?"

"Hand me my white coat," she said, barely a whisper.

Grant grabbed her white coat—surprisingly heavy —from the back of the chair and handed it to her.

"Thanks." She fished a couple of gloves out of an inside pocket and drew them on with trembling hands.

Hope examined the envelope and carefully slit it open. She pressed knuckles to her mouth, the other hand on her stomach.

"You okay?" He stepped closer.

The same damned thing—glued mismatched letters spelled out,

I KNOW WHERE YOU LIVE.

Not the brightest bulb, since the delivery made that obvious. Perfect to make her worry, though. Did the bastard get off on that?

Beside him, Hope swayed, and Grant slid an arm around her waist. "Hey, sit down." He led her to the chair and set aside her coat. "What's up with the letter?"

"I don't know. It's the third one." She turned wide eyes to him but managed to smile. "I'm sure it's just a sick prank. But it kind of freaks me out—what if it's true, that someone's watching me?"

Damn, she really does need Mojo.

Grant hesitated, hating to set her up for disappointment, then asked, "Are you going to call the cops?"

"No. The hospital discouraged it. Didn't want the publicity."

Bastards. Grant tried to make it better. "Doubt the police would've done anything with it, anyway. Some of these small-town cops are more about posing and hair gel than investigation. They might even think you wrote it yourself, to gain attention."

"What?" She scowled at him.

"I know you didn't." He held up his hands and tried again. "Anonymous letter-writers are usually just cowards. People with true intent to harm don't hide or forewarn."

She grimaced, unconvinced. "Or he's just getting started. What if he's been inside when no one was home?"

"Nah, not with Mojo on the case. But let's check. Do you have any more gloves?"

Grant put on a pair and grabbed the letter. "Magazines have a characteristic smell, from the inks they favor and any samples they contain—colognes and such."

He held the letter out to the Malinois. "Mojo, *find.*"

The dog carefully snuffed the sheet and envelope, then trailed Grant around the room as he walked backwards in the "Lackland shuffle," his hand going low, then high, then low again, followed by Mojo's nose, as they traveled the perimeter. "If he finds something, he'll signal me. But no one with that scent's been through your door or window."

"Thank you." She tried to smile.

Grant paused. "Want me to sweep your bedroom?"

Not the way he'd wanted to get there, but it might bring her peace of mind, and he couldn't deny the jolt of curiosity, despite the circumstances.

Her breasts rose with her deep sigh, and he found himself holding his breath.

"Okay." Hope sighed. "It does have a window." She made no move to follow them.

He took Mojo down the hall to the bathroom, then her bedroom. Grant stepped over a pile of clothes by the door and caught a subtle scent of green apple. An unmade bed, dog hair on the left side.

"Lucky bastard," he muttered.

He glanced at the closet as Mojo sniffed his way past. Folded jeans and T-shirts on the shelf. No-nonsense business clothes, and a couple of strappy dresses, one with a ruffled hem.

Sensible shoes lined the closet floor—and one pair of sexy black high heels. *Hell, yeah.* He'd love to see her in that dress—or maybe just the shoes.

Grant smiled. If she had a boyfriend here—or probably at all—she wouldn't be letting Mojo sleep on the bed.

Focus, you moron, he chided himself.

Grant moved along the wall, paying careful attention to the window, and glanced at the bed again. "I might have to take your spot, bro," he said, and Mojo wagged.

They walked back out to the kitchen. "All clear."

"Thanks." Hope sighed, closing her eyes, and something stirred in his chest.

Her pulse beat in her neck, and he imagined the feel of it under his lips.

"No problem. He'll remember the scent, too, even later."

18
Savage
-GRANT-

O ut of excuses to stall, Grant moved to the couch to get his bag. "I guess I'd better get going."

"Thanks for watching him—I was really worried." Hope flushed, as if unused to asking for help.

"No problem. I'll do anything for Mojo. Besides…" Grant hesitated, then shrugged. "I've been sleeping in my vehicle."

It was worth the hit to his pride to assuage hers.

"What?" She raised her eyebrows, her hands on nice hips. "Why, exactly, do you think Baby's better off with you, if you're homeless?"

So much for full disclosure.

"It's not what you think," he retorted. "I just couldn't get in anywhere on short notice. I dropped *everything* when I heard he was here. *That's* why he's better off with me."

She blinked.

Shit. Should have left it alone. But this woman pushed buttons he didn't even know he had.

Grant tried to salvage it. "It was great to see him again."

He picked up his bag, sick at the thought of leaving Mojo.

"Wait."

Grant turned.

Hope bit her lip, rubbing at a scratch on the table. She raised her eyes to his. "Do you mind staying? Just for a few days?"

She took a deep breath and rushed on. "Since you have no place to sleep. You can take the bedroom and I'll move to the couch. I—"

"No problem," he said, too fast. The woman intrigued him.

Stop it. You're here for your dog.

"Oh, thank you. You're sure?"

"Yeah. But you don't need to give up your bed."

When she bit her lip, he suppressed a grin and changed the subject.

"So, it looks like joint custody, then?"

"A temporary thing, no more." Hope smoothed her scowl. "I do appreciate it, though," she said stiffly. "Your staying."

"What can I say? You made me an offer I can't *defuse*."

Her quick smile warmed him, before she squelched it, substituting an eye roll. "Yeah. It's business: your visibility and help with Baby, in trade for a nice place to stay and time with your former pet."

Pet?

But she'd tipped her hand when she smiled at his pun, so instead of taking offense, Grant joked, "Unless you change your mind about sleeping arrangements."

Shit, too fast.

She raised an eyebrow. "What makes you think that'll happen?" Her gaze darted to his lips.

"I'm an EOD tech. That means I'm *dynamite*."

Grant smiled, waiting to see if she'd flare up, ignore it, or take the bait. Signal that he could kiss her, but she gave him nothing.

He shook his head as if astonished. "You're saying 'no' to friends with benefits?"

Hope snorted. "For that, we'd have to be *friends*. I've got to get to work, Captain Dynamite."

She headed to the bathroom, and the shower started.

"Damn." Grant shook his head again. "That woman is savage, Mojo, but she needs us. No one will get past us, huh, boy?"

Grant scratched Mojo's ears and ruefully eyed the package of buns on the countertop.

"I guess now I'll have to eat some of your damned hot dogs."

19
So-Called Charm

-HOPE-

*H*ope re-secured her ponytail and shrugged on her white coat. She slipped into the ER physician's staff lounge in search of a cold drink before her shift.

Clay and Joanna sat at one of the round laminate tables, him reading *The Wall Street Journal* with his chair tipped back, her scrolling through her phone.

"Hey, guys," Hope said.

It can't be them.

Clay's chair thumped down. "Dr. Hernandez. Any news from your stalker?"

Great, when Koonce asked me not to talk about it.

She sat in the chair between them with a nonchalant smile. "Got another letter that said, "'I know where you live.'"

Clay rolled his eyes. "No rocket scientist, I guess."

He had a point. It was almost laughable, to think

either of her educated colleagues would send something so inane.

Joanna's eyes narrowed. "Now what?"

Hope shrugged. "Koonce discouraged me from going to the police or talking about it. Doesn't want bad publicity for the Med Cen."

"Maybe you should anyway," Joanna said.

Is she trying to trip me up?

Clay said, "No, he's right. In a small town like this, things get around. Besides, what could they do, with no crime committed?"

"Get a restraining order, if they found the guy?" Joanna asked.

"I don't know." Hope watched for their reactions. "Even if they ID'd the guy and issued one, how many times do you read about men hurting the women they stalk, even with a restraining order? I think those only work on people who have a degree of restraint to begin with."

"True." Joanna grimaced.

Clay frowned. He'd been complacent about the job, confident in his abilities—and connections, but he did seem to care about her safety.

"The good thing is, Baby's former owner is staying with me, helping watch my dog, so I'll be able to make all my shifts."

Hope smiled as if they'd be happy for her.

Clay raised an eyebrow. "You're sure about this guy moving in? You barely know him—what if *he's* your stalker? Didn't he show up right before the letters started?"

"I'm sure."

Joanna's eyes searched hers as if trying to gauge her fear. "Are you okay? It must be awful, every day wondering if you're being watched. Analyzing every interaction to see who's a suspect—patients, staff, the guy at the gas station." She shook her head. "I don't know if I could live like that."

Was Joanna trying to run her off? The woman was right, though—long term, it wouldn't be worth it if the letters kept up. There would be other jobs, other towns, though Hope had dreamed of working here.

She pushed her worries aside, headed to the ER, and concentrated on battling death.

"Nice job with that chest tube," Chen told her at the end of shift.

When he left, Joanna said, "You got all the good cases tonight."

For a change. "There's always tomorrow, right?" Hope laughed but she'd already begun to dread the long walk out to the parking lot.

Light glimmered on dark empty vehicles. Head up, keys protruding from between her fingers, Hope strode with purpose to her Jeep, peering in before she unlocked it, listening hard for someone sneaking up behind her. Should she take a circuitous route home?

Her eyes darted to the headlights behind her on the drive.

"I know where you live."

What if he were waiting for her at home?

Grant's pickup in front of the house eased her mind, though he could be out walking Baby. He did love the dog—she had to give him that.

She opened the door to the sound of savage snarling.

Shit!

A man lay on the floor, Baby growling above him, ripping at the arms raised to protect his face.

Hope gasped. *The stalker?*

She lunged for the baseball bat in the umbrella stand and whirled. "Baby, stop!"

"All done." A breathless male voice.

Grant's voice.

Baby dropped to his belly, tail wagging.

Grant sat up, laughing, and dropped the frayed rope—that was what Baby had been savaging. "Hey, Hope. Didn't hear you come in."

His eyes widened when he saw the baseball bat. "Jesus. You were going to club me?" He grabbed the happy dog's ruff and shook it, breathing hard, his forearm muscles flexing.

She dropped the bat, her face warm. "I thought Baby caught the stalker." Who'd have expected someone to be rolling around on the floor with their dog?

My dog, she corrected herself.

"If he comes around, he's toast. We've got your back." Grant's promise felt real, a simple fact. He waved to the couch, casually proud. "Sit and eat a decent meal. I made spaghetti."

Hope sank down and put up her tired feet, suppressing a groan.

Grant brought her reheated carbonara and sat beside her. "Tell me about your day, dear." He grinned.

"Can't. Not much, anyway. Patient confidentiality." Hope shrugged. "I think I'm making progress—there are two other residents who want the spot, and one's the sort who thinks he's God's gift." She raised an eyebrow and Grant laughed.

"Yeah. The type who has a hard time getting smacked down." His smile said, *not me.*

"How'd it go at the festival?" she asked.

Grant regaled her with stories of fussy rabbit show contestants, devious bluegrass fans, and lost children.

"Sounds hectic," she said. "I'd love to see The Whiskey Barrels, though."

"Maybe you can," he said.

Would he want to go with me? Her idiotic heart skipped. "Not likely, with my hours."

It won't be forever, she reminded herself. But it would be long enough that, flirty or not, Grant would tire of waiting for her and lose interest. Why did that bother her?

"Wouldn't have figured you for a country fan." He appraised her, head tilted. "All that drawling and twanging."

"It's not all like that."

She frowned, trying to articulate why she loved country music. "It's not pretentious. The songs have *heart*. They're about something real: love and loss. Regret and anger. Why do you think The Whiskey Barrels are so popular?"

Grant snorted. "Because they look like a boy band kept in cold storage, and trotted out dressed in denim and cowboy hats?"

"Says the mall cop," Hope snickered and finished her pasta. "Thanks." She held her empty plate out to Baby.

Grant's eyebrows shot up. "You let him lick the plates? Here."

He took her dish to the sink, shaking his head. "You're spoiling him. Bacon, sleeping on the bed…"

Hope's laugh turned into a yawn. "I love him. He deserves it."

Grant sat down again, lean hands rubbing the dog's ears, and gave her a smile.

Baby's tail thumped her shins.

Hope relaxed, into the feeling of safety, as if Grant had soothed the knots from her neck. Almost like they were a family. "Want to watch TV?" she asked, just to prolong the truce.

They settled in, but the tryptophan rush from eating hit her like a truck and she kept nodding off.

Her head jerked her out of a dead sleep.

What were they watching? Some monster movie with *worms?* "I can't stay awake. Sorry. Goodnight. Come on, Baby."

Despite Grant's protests that it was early, her dog happily followed her and leapt up onto the bed. Hope brushed her teeth, imagining Grant stretched on the couch in the next room.

She slept better that night than she had in a week. Exhaustion, or knowing that two hundred sixty pounds of combined human and canine muscle had her back?

Yet in the morning, she found Baby sleeping on the floor next to Grant, whose sculpted chest rose and fell. One hand rested on the dog's ruff.

"Traitor," she murmured, and started coffee instead of ogling Grant. She would *not* look to see if he had the physiologic morning erection typical of young males.

"Hey, Pretty Girl." His sleep-hoarsened voice came from behind her. He sat up, sheets safely bunched around his hips.

He looked big and male and delectable in an unscripted, genuine way. He bent to scratch one shin, revealing scars from knee to ankle—shrapnel?

"Why do you call me that?" She pressed her lips together and concentrated on spooning sugar into her mug.

"Pretty Girl?" Grant frowned. "It just popped into my mind when I saw you, and sort of stuck. I had no idea you were a doctor. And you are pretty."

"Thanks, but 'girl' is a little dismissive, don't you think?"

"No. I really don't—to me, it means 'young woman.' Nothing insulting there at all, but I'll stop if you want. I also call you 'Doc,' and 'Hope,' if you hadn't noticed."

He stood and stretched, and the sunlight caught his blue gym shorts, stretched across his trapped erection.

Oh, my. Hope averted her eyes and poured coffee.

"What *do* you want me to call you?" Grant ambled toward her, unconcerned.

"Hope is fine. I guess the other's okay, too, but I'll

have to call you Captain Dynamite." She held up the pot. "Coffee?"

"Sure. Black, please." He accepted a stoneware mug, took a sip, and set it on the countertop. "Let me tend to my dog."

Hope put her hands on her hips. *"Your* dog?"

Grant chuckled, then pointed to the dog door. "Mojo, go *unload.*"

Baby ducked through the exit and Hope choked on her coffee.

Grant raised an eyebrow. "You okay, Doc?"

"Yes." She cleared her throat. "Does 'unload' mean what I think it does?"

Grant laughed. "Probably. If they learn to eliminate on command, it saves all kinds of problems when you take them out, whether on a mission or to the store."

"Wish I'd known."

His eyes lit with curiosity, and when she told the story, he roared. "He's well-trained, you have to admit. You just have to know the magic words. They should have told you, but I guess—"

He frowned, abruptly changing course—why?

"You'll learn," he said, "but some of it might be the hard way. Starting fresh with a new dog would be easier. No surprises." He rubbed a hand over his stubble, and she wondered what it would feel like against her skin.

Talk about a surprise—why was she thinking about him that way, this guy who wanted to take her dog?

Grant smiled at her. "It'd be *Staff Sergeant* Dynamite, by the way, not Captain. Since we're talking proper forms of address. That was my rank, before I... left." His Adam's apple bobbed and his gaze turned to Baby again.

Hope dished up the dog's food while Grant watched as if assessing her, but he gave a nod when she finished and said, *"Go ahead"* to release him. She glanced at the sofa, strewn with rumpled sheets.

Grant stripped the bedclothes, folding them neatly, while she sat.

"I gotta ask. Why *Baby?*" Dark eyes held hers. "It's such a pansy name for a badass military dog. *Mojo's* a name for a hero."

"It's a term of endearment, for someone beloved." She glared at him. "I guess you've never gotten that or you'd understand." Crap, that was harsh.

"No, I haven't." He carefully finished his folding. "But—"

"I didn't mean—"

"—I'm working on it now." Grinning, he picked up his coffee cup and sauntered over to sit next to her.

Hope laughed. "Good luck with that."

"It's not luck. It's persistence, optimism and worth." Grant shrugged. "Already we've gone from strangers to enemies to joint K9 custodians to roommates, in less than one week. That's even before I unleash my charm. Just wait 'til you get to know the real me."

He *was* charming. Charming enough to tempt her.

"Yeah? You've already told me the objective of your charm offensive is Baby."

"I've got no secrets." His eyes were steady on her, and her pulse kicked up. "I'm here for my dog, whatever it takes."

Strange, the disappointment that pricked her heart.

Grant leaned forward and brushed her hair back from her face. "But that doesn't mean he's all I want."

Her breath came short, and she stared at him. "It's a bad idea, friends with benefits."

"Why?"

"Because it's one-sided. You'd get a boink buddy and be gone."

"You'd get a boink buddy, too." His smile was puzzled.

"Uh-huh."

Grant's eyebrows shot up at her dismissive tone. "Wait, you don't like sex? Are you *ace* or something?"

"No, I'm not asexual, and I do like sex, but it's overrated, frankly."

"What?" His surprise seemed real. "How can you say that?"

"It just ... is." Her face warmed.

"I don't get how..." He frowned. "Wait, they didn't take care of you? Did you fake it? Because otherwise no man would stop until you were satisfied."

"No, I didn't fake it!" she snapped, then shrugged. "Less than twenty percent of women climax with penetration alone." *Geez, stop being so medical.* "And yes, they did stop. They just ... assumed, and by then I was fine with that." At a certain point, it wasn't worth it.

Why am I even having this conversation?

"Then they were dicks," Grant said, his voice laced with disgust. He shook his head. "That's a crime."

His eyes dropped to her lips, and he set his coffee down, leaning closer. "Let's change that—your stats. When do you have to be at work, Pretty Girl?"

Oh, God. Hope swallowed, tempted. Her heart pounded and desire pooled low in her pelvis, a traitorous warmth that cared nothing about his transience or ridiculous nicknames, only his sex appeal.

But he'd told her flat-out that Baby was his goal, and she'd be just a bonus.

To hell with that. He's getting neither.

Hope smiled. "Not until two. But I need to clean the bathroom."

Surprise flickered across his arrogant, handsome face.

She walked out of the room. *Stupid Sergeant Dynamite and his so-called charm.*

Black Sheep

-GRANT-

"*D*amn, that was cold," Grant told Mojo, as he watched Hope walk away, her sleep shirt barely covering her ass, those long legs flashing.

She flipped heavy black hair over her shoulder, and it swayed in counterpoint to the thin cotton hem, mesmerizing.

"Never thought I'd rate lower than scrubbing toilets."

And now that she was in the bathroom, he couldn't do anything to relieve his hard-on. *Distraction it is.* "I want my *rope*," he told Mojo, but really, it was Hope he wanted.

How could a man let a woman like that go unsatisfied?

The dog pranced up with his prize, and they went into the backyard. A fierce tug-of-war ensued, until Hope sauntered out to watch, this time wearing tight jeans and a T-shirt loose enough to drape down over the curves beneath, modest yet maddening.

She sat on the shabby porch swing, one leg tucked underneath, the other bare foot touching the decking.

"All done," he told Mojo.

The dog released the rope, panting, and leaped up next to Hope on the swing.

"He ditched you fast." She laughed at Grant and rubbed Mojo's ears.

Grant had never imagined he could feel so envious of a dog. "You let him sit on the furniture *and* sleep on the bed? That is one lucky dog." He contented himself with leaning against the porch support.

"Yep," she said, smug, as she sipped coffee. "My house, my rules. And there's no risk to him here. Nothing dangerous. I hope that'll give you peace once you move on."

Damn, why was she so prickly now? He'd thought they were making progress, but she was pushing him out the door. *Serves me right for getting sidetracked.*

"Peace? Thinking about all his hours alone? I know you love him, but a dog needs time, and you have so little." Surely she'd be reasonable.

"Lots of working people have dogs," she coolly replied. "Besides, ER work is shift work with reasonable hours, just as soon as I graduate. And what about you? Your security job has long hours, too, I'll bet."

"I only took this gig while I hunted down Mojo." Too late, he realized his mistake.

"Oh? That means you'll be homeless *and* unemployed?" She snorted. "You're not exactly selling it, here."

"I'm not selling anything. I'll do whatever it takes, then go back home, where I have family and friends to help out."

Did she flinch at that? Never a good idea to disclose everything—why had he?

Hope tossed her head. "What about a new dog for *you*, then? Since you have so much time and support?"

Jesus. She didn't get it at all, the idea of loyalty and partnership?

Grant sank to the floor, and Mojo hopped down and put his head on Grant's thigh. "I owe him," he said, voice low. "He saved my life, and hundreds more."

Her expression sobered, her lip drawn between her teeth. "I found out a little about what happened. I can't imagine..." She glanced at Mojo. "What made you become a bomb tech, anyway?"

"It sounds so corny." Grant sighed. "Let's go down to the park and I'll tell you."

"The park?"

She didn't get out at all? "There's one three blocks south. Come on. It'll be good for you. Mojo loves to show off." Grant waved a Kong at Mojo, who yelped and spun when he saw the knobby rubber toy.

Hope smiled. "Okay."

They leashed up Mojo and walked toward the little fenced park. The dog paced happily between them to an empty soccer field and playground.

Grant closed the gate, unclipped Mojo, and sent the Kong downrange. "I wanted to be a hero. To make a difference." He shrugged, watching the dog streak after the toy. "Instead, I'm the black sheep. My folks wanted me to join the family law firm. My brother still practices in Broken Arrow, near Tulsa."

Mojo raced back to return the Kong to Grant.

"I get the hero thing. But bombs?"

"It was that or be suspended." Enjoying the cease-fire, Grant laughed at her puzzlement and hurled the Kong. "I was a bit of a handful as a kid—nothing bad, just pranks. A gamer, a geek—in Robotics Lab, all that. Bad grades in everything but math and science. Not the son my parents wanted, for sure."

The corners of her mouth lifted. How would she react to the whole truth?

"Anyway, junior year, we were playing our biggest football rivals at their homecoming. We had a great team, with a real chance of going to the state championship. I rigged up this little surprise in an empty popcorn drum. Hid it in the trash can near their end zone. An air cannon."

Her eyes widened.

Grant shrugged and threw again. "I made sure no one was anywhere near—had a radio remote. They were about to crown the homecoming king and queen and BAM! Blew a big mushroom cloud of blue and white confetti—our school colors. It was epic."

"It didn't go over well?"

He barked a laugh. "No, that's for damned sure. I was so dumb—hadn't figured it'd scare people. They locked everything down and searched the grounds. My school chose to forfeit.

I thought it'd be a cool display of school spirit, but the girls were furious that someone disrupted the crowning—nothing compared to how pissed the boys were at losing the chance to go to state. I felt like shit."

Grant rubbed his forehead. "I'd worked alone and figured I was safe, but the second my older brother heard, he asked, 'What the hell were you thinking?' and walked away. All weekend I prayed and sweated —my dad would have killed me. I heard nothing but anger and disgust from other kids. I went in Monday to confess to Principal Stanton, knowing my life was over."

"What did he do?"

"She. Stanton listened and thanked me for saving her the trouble—said she knew it was me the second it happened. Then she asked, 'What was the risk of an accidental triggering if someone had an RC airplane nearby? What damage could it have caused to someone's eyes or hearing, if they'd been close? How do you think the football team feels, and the band and coaches? All those parents? What harm will this cause your father's firm if this gets out?'"

Even now, nausea stirred at the memory. "It was terrible; I threw up in her office. Told her I never meant for any of that to happen, that it wasn't a real explosive, that I'd made sure no one was hurt, but she said, 'Doesn't matter—it *did* hurt.' I waited for her to suspend me. For the whole school to turn against me and my parents to take my car keys."

"Sounds awful." Hope's eyes were sympathetic.

"Instead, Stanton gave me a choice—suspension, or a research paper and oral report on explosive devices: their history and dangers, current use and mitigation. My parents were so proud, the way I buckled down that week."

Grant gave a terse laugh at the irony. "Learned all about mines, World War II bombs, IEDs, demolition, and bomb squads. I went back to present my work and when I was done, she said, 'You're a smart guy, Mr. Calloway, with a bright future—unless you screw it up. Who do you choose to be—a screwup, or a hero?'"

He shrugged and signaled *all done* to the panting dog. "The rest is history. I found a way to blow shit up for fun *and* save people." He bent to shake the dog's ruff. "All I have to decide is if I'll still do bomb work, security, or train dogs or techs, versus law school. So, employment won't be an issue."

"Isn't it terrifying, to dispose of a bomb?" Hope tilted her head. "I doubt you can trust the robots entirely, nor any equipment."

"You trust your dog."

Mojo flopped onto his back, wriggling on the grass like a puppy, legs waving in the air, tongue lolling.

Grant said, "But no, the bomb suit won't protect you from a close-up blast. You're either right, or it's no longer your problem. At zero range, you wouldn't have time to feel it. Farther out, you might survive but lose your hands, since you can't wear gloves for some of it. You kind of get in the zone, where you have a job to do and that's all that matters."

"Sounds like medicine, during a code or a bad trauma." She eyed him with—respect?

That felt like warm sunshine, after the way he'd been denigrated at Spotlight, and he really enjoyed talking with her. At the very least, she might come to understand the bond he shared with Mojo.

The dog walked up and laid his chin on her leg, tail wagging.

Grant watched the breeze stir her long hair, and longing stirred in his chest.

Hell, best case, he might share a bond with her over time. He'd joked about joint custody, but what if it could become a reality? She needed a decent man: someone to support her, protect her, and he'd not felt like this in... well, ever.

There's no rush to leave town.

The truth was, he had no place else he'd rather be.

No Miracle

-HOPE-

*T*hursday night, Dr. Chen assigned Hope to a fresh heart attack—flattering, but scary: an MI could go south so easily, but adrenaline and training served her well as she treated Mr. Hall, an elderly out-of-town cancer patient here to check "peak-bagging" with his grandson off his bucket list.

What possessed people to climb mountains at all, let alone someone ill?

Pressure's holding, but his sats are tenuous. The green tracings wavered.

The hipster kid clasped the frail man's shoulder. "You got this, Gramps. We have two peaks left, you know." He smiled at Hope. "I couldn't keep up with him."

She checked her patient's ankles for edema.

Watery blue eyes met hers, trusting. White hair stood up in tufts, disheveled by the clear venti-mask.

"Three out of five's not bad," he rasped, winking at Hope. "We'll see if—"

He slumped as the tracing widened to jagged spikes.

V tach.

Shit! Hope reached for his neck—no pulse. "I need the cart!" she cried, and the nurse ripped the curtain open. "Wait outside," Hope told the grandson, and started CPR until the crash cart arrived.

Personnel rushed in, and Hope administered the first shock—unsuccessful. "I need epinephrine, 1 mg IV." She designated roles: "Take over CPR" and "I need you to record and keep time" and "No pulse? Everybody clear" before she discharged a second shock.

Nothing.

"Resume CPR." There was a chance, however slim. Hope ran the code, grimly determined.

Chen strolled in.

Oh, thank God.

"How can I help, Dr. Hernandez?" He gazed at her, impassive.

Shit! He's leaving it to me? "We've got it covered." She shoved down despair; the odds were miniscule that the man would survive. "Can you update the grandson in ten minutes? I think we'd better hang some crepe." Kindest to prepare the guy for the worst. The line between therapy and torment was so hazy.

But he was strong enough to climb mountains. It's worth a shot. "I need 300 milligrams of amiodarone IV."

The tracing flatlined. *Asystole. Shit!* "Continue compressions. Let's give another milligram of epinephrine IV."

Time narrowed.

Hope ran the algorithms of the code—an exercise in futility. Defeat solidified, a leaden weight in her chest. "Time, please?"

"Twenty-eight minutes," said the timekeeper.

Well past the twelve-minute average of a successful resuscitation. Sadness welled but Hope still had responsibilities. Time to take care of her team, who'd need reassurance they'd done everything, without a gruesome prolongation. "We'll do one more round of epi, then call it." She caught the eye of Dr. Chen, who nodded almost imperceptibly.

As expected, there was no miracle.

Hope called the code and thanked the team. "Good job, everyone." They slipped away, leaving her alone with her patient. She caught up his bony hand. "I'm sorry," she whispered.

The curtain slid open. "That was well-run," said Joanna. She paused. "You okay?"

Hope tried to smile. "Yeah. Thanks. I'd better go talk with his grandson."

She braced herself and entered the tiny consultation room.

Bleak eyes turned to her, and he covered his face with his hands. "Oh, God. Shit, shit."

"I'm so sorry," she said. "We did everything we could."

The young man's knuckles whitened as he clasped his hands. "I know you did," he said brokenly. "And I know he was sick, but... I just can't believe it. He looked so strong on Homestake Peak." He shook his head.

"I'll bet he wouldn't have wished for anything different than to spend time with his grandson." However sincere, it sounded lame.

"Probably not." He laughed through tears as the charge nurse knocked. "But we had a bargain, and he's not getting out of it. Once this is all over, I'll carry his ashes up Mount Alice and Bellevue Mountain. Thanks for everything, Doctor."

He stood to follow the nurse to say his goodbyes.

Hope's heart squeezed, and she finished her notes and dictation.

"Go home, Hope," Chen said from the doorway.

Crap! Had she—

"You did a great job, but it's tough on a person. Go home and I'll see you tomorrow."

Hope managed to hold it together as she gathered

her things and drove home. She slipped in quietly without turning on the light, yet Baby's cold nose pressed into her hand, his tail waving: Love and acceptance, despite what happened.

A lump rose in her throat.

Grant's deep voice floated over, hoarse with sleep. "Hey. Didn't think you'd be back 'til two."

The lump in her throat sharpened, and she couldn't speak.

"Doc?" Grant turned on the lamp and sat up, his eyes concerned. "Hey, Pretty Girl. What's wrong?"

She turned away. "I... can't talk about it."

The couch creaked.

"Hey," he said, right behind her. He turned her to him and slid his arms around her. "It's tough, saving the world. Sometimes, it doesn't work out, even when we do our best."

His gentle tone breached her shield.

Hope clung to him and wept.

Grant held her, patient. No hurry, no judgement. Like he really got it.

She gradually became aware of his wet shirt. "Sorry," she said. "Let me— "

"Shh. Just sit." He led her to the couch, and she sank into the nest of blankets, scented with Grant's woodsy cologne. He brought her a glass of water, sat next to her, and pulled her into his arms. "Just breathe."

His heart thumped below her cheek, steady, as her sadness drained into him.

"Thank you," she finally whispered. Hiccupping, she went to bed, Baby padding behind her.

The Whiskey Barrels

-GRANT-

*T*he next day, country music surrounded Grant, and the percentage of cowboy hats in the crowd increased. No country fan, but he had to admit that some of the tunes were catchy. Making the rounds of the east parking lot, he heard a panicked female voice.

"—away from me! I mean it!"

Grant ran in that direction.

Three men had a brunette in a Stetson and band T-shirt backed against a pickup. The tallest guy leaned in. "Darlin', you have a better shot with a real man than those Whiskey Barrel pansies. I promise, I'm a whole barrel of fun."

Grant strode over. "Ma'am, is this *barrel of fun* bothering you?"

"Barrel of monkeys, more like," she spat.

The men broke apart, hands spread. "We ain't doing nothing—"

She crossed her arms and glared, then spoke to Grant. "My boyfriend's with the band and I need to find him."

"I'll take you." Grant turned to the dipshits. "Out. Now."

""Blow me," the ringleader grumbled. "This is bullshit. We'll get your bitch ass fired, you faggot."

"Go ahead," said Grant. "The name's Calloway."

The guys glared at him but walked out the exit gate, muttering.

"Thank you," the lady said. "My boyfriend's the drummer for The Whiskey Barrels."

Grant keyed his walkie talkie and called the secure VIP lot, confirming they knew her. "Come on."

He walked her over to a huge, gleaming RV painted with the band logo. When he knocked, the door burst open and the band came out. One swept her into a hug.

Grant studied the other band members as they shook his hand. Did Hope have a celebrity crush on one of them? All of them? God knows he'd overheard some weird shit from fans this week.

They seemed like ordinary Southern guys, though it was strange to hear the British accent of the redheaded guitarist. Then again, it wasn't like he'd be singing. Yet he was the one the women swooned over: him and the lead singer, Hardy West—like *that* wasn't an obvious stage name.

Grant had heard a few of their songs this week—the festival was a damned crash course in All Things Country—but some of them weren't bad. A shame Hope's shift kept her from seeing them perform.

"Hey, thanks for intervening," said West. "Let me give you a couple tickets to the show."

"No, thanks." At the guy's frown, Grant added, "I couldn't use them; my girlfriend's working tonight. I was glad to help."

Girlfriend sounded good. Could he make that happen? *I'll buy her a CD, at least.* He kicked himself for not getting one for her earlier; he'd lost his chance to get it autographed.

His radio squawked. "Yo, Captain DB, where are you?"

Great. Givens always wanted him to tag along at the pre-show briefing. Grant excused himself and went to meet his supervisor outside the food pavilion, enduring his piggy-eyed once-over. *I'll stay in the background.* No need to mention he'd already met the band.

"Let's go, Captain DB," Givens said.

Grant followed the man's sweating back to the

VIP lot. The man hefted his belly above his low-slung belt. "I'll do the talking."

Fine by me. Grant adopted a look of studious respect as his boss knocked on the door, introduced himself, and briefed the musicians on emergency procedures.

West smiled broadly as he interrupted Givens. "I want to thank you boys for coming down. It's been real helpful." He strutted over with a couple of tickets and gave them to Grant's boss, then shut the door.

Givens eyed Grant with pity. "Maybe next year you'll rate, DB."

23
Hope Succumbs

-HOPE-

*A*s time rolled past, Hope had to admit it was good to have Grant around. His work hours were more regular than hers. Baby was happy, Grant was a decent cook, and he straightened up a little, too. Was it a commentary on her hours and lifestyle?

No. He's never been judgmental about that. He probably did it as payment, because she'd refused the rent he'd tried to give her.

The letters continued yet Grant made her feel safe at night, though sometimes she tossed and turned, thinking of him lying on the narrow couch, nothing between them but a door and a couple layers of cotton. Hope was tempted to walk into the living room and slide beneath the thin sheet.

Which was stupid—the same old promise of sex, always disappointing in the end. Still, every glance, every word from him thrilled her, though she knew it was nothing but chemicals interacting with neurons.

Yet the sexual attraction couldn't account for the way he made her laugh. How great it was to have someone to talk to who could talk back—and talk back he did, teasing her and keeping her grounded. Someone who was there, without belittling her accomplishments to satisfy his own ego.

Figures. The one good man I run into is only temporary.

On Thursday, the mail thumped into the slot and Hope approached, steeling herself.

Sure enough, there was another one, with a local postmark:

DO YOU SLEEP NAKED?

Her skin crawled. She glanced around, but Baby stretched and yawned, unconcerned. *Thank God for him.*

And Grant. Hope eyed the clock. He'd be home soon, with a few hours' overlap before she had to leave.

The door opened as Grant's deep voice reverberated. "Hey, it's me. I brought us ice cream."

Baby leaped up, whirling in joy.

Feeling much the same way, suddenly breathless, Hope said, "Hi. I've got supper, if you want."

"Yes, ma'am." He blinked when he saw the hot dogs. Maybe because it was the third time this week?

"Thanks. I'll cook tomorrow." Grant bent to greet Baby.

Her phone chimed and she jumped.

Grant eyed her. "Any new letters?"

She put a pint of mint chocolate chip into the freezer. "Yeah. This one said, **'Do you sleep naked?'**"

"Damn, that's vile." He sat, waiting politely for her.

She waved for him to go ahead and eat.

He reached for a hot dog and grimaced. "It's possible the police could get prints. If it's someone with a record, they might talk to him—or her—for a pretty girl."

He smiled at his obvious attempt to rile her, but sobered when she only hugged herself, shivering. "But you'll never get a restraining order. My brother says for that there has to be an immediate, credible threat."

A credible threat.

The guy texting in the hospital parking lot? The cashier who leered at her? Hope's stomach flipped.

"Hey, Pretty Girl." Grant took her hand and nodded at the dog. "Nothing's going to happen to you with us around."

Baby wagged in agreement, and her worry subsided.

"Thanks," Hope said. "I can't go to the police, anyway. I want this job, and the hospital CEO made it clear I can't make waves."

"You don't think that's a bad sign? You'd work at a place like that?" He loaded his hot dog with mustard, took a bite, and swallowed. "You could get a job anywhere. I have a lot of military connections, if that would help."

Another chomp—he must really love hot dogs.

"Maybe. But I don't want 'anywhere.' I want some place I can get out and do things."

His lips curved. "'Do things.' Like what?"

He licked mustard from his thumb, dark eyes on hers, and her insides melted.

She'd like to do all sorts of things with him. Suddenly, eating a hot dog in front of him seemed obscene. Cheeks warm, she called Baby over and gave him the rest of it.

Grant opened his mouth.

Hope hurried on before he could comment. "Maybe learn to snowboard."

"Mmm." He stared at her as if he knew her inner thoughts before he shook himself. "Sounds fun."

Grant finished off his hot dog and rolled his neck. "So does ice cream." He got the pint from the freezer and two spoons.

She hesitated at the intimacy, but dipped in. Maybe that would cool her off.

His molten gaze followed the utensil from the carton to her mouth, and he took a bite while she tried to tear her eyes away from him licking the spoon.

Hope floundered. "You know, the couch wouldn't bother me much, since I'm smaller. You should switch with me, if your neck's stiff. You've been a godsend, staying here, and—"

"Not my neck." His mouth twitched—or had she imagined it? "But I won't take the bed. Not unless it's shared."

His slow smile made her pulse kick up.

"Oh, it would be—Baby sleeps there."

Grant's eyes widened. His face fell, though he recovered fast, laughing. "Not what I had in mind."

Hope's stomach fluttered. "I guess we could do like in that old movie, and each keep one foot on the floor."

"No problem." Grant set down the ice cream and stood, holding out his hand.

Oh, my God—he wants to go now? Heat gathered in her pelvis, her body completely in favor of the idea. "I don't think you get it. Their feet were on opposite sides of the bed." She ignored his hand.

"Let's go. I'll take that challenge. It sounds like fun."

Hope frowned—was she missing something?

Grant eased back down into his chair, his voice husky. "I don't think you could do it for long, though. One leg down, with me next to you? You have no idea how far I can reach, and still keep one foot on the floor."

"Oh…" Her mind ran riot, her temperature rising, and she swallowed. "Never mind, then."

If he was disappointed, he didn't show it. "Maybe we could share the couch instead." He brushed his thumb along her bottom lip, got up, pulled the drapes, and crossed to the sofa. "Come on, Pretty Girl."

Baby lay next to the coffee table, at Grant's feet.

Hope couldn't resist. She sank down beside him, heart thumping. "You know, we share the couch every day."

"It'll be different tonight," Grant promised as he interlaced his fingers with hers. "I wanted to kiss you from the moment I saw you." He pressed his lips onto her knuckles, his eyes intent.

She wanted it, too. *But he's leaving…* "I said you wouldn't be getting me naked."

"You did." He ran his fingers through her hair, stopping short of her breast, and her nipples tightened. "And I'll respect that, if that's what you still want. But you'd be surprised at what I can do even without you naked." His heated gaze burned into her.

What I want.

Grant tipped her face up and kissed her.

Hope closed her eyes and gave in to sensation: warm, firm lips, the tickle of his stubble, his breath feathering her cheek. She slid hands up his hard pecs to his shoulders. Naked, with him?

I do want it.

His kiss deepened, his fingers cupping the back of her head. His tongue slipped between her lips, offering the taste of mint and chocolate, and her mouth tingled, breath coming short. Grant's hand splayed across her back, pulling her closer.

Back muscles flexed under her fingertips, and she dipped beneath his T-shirt hem, eager to feel skin.

Grant broke from her, breathing hard. In one smooth motion, he reached behind his head, yanked off his shirt, and threw it onto the coffee table.

"*I've* got no issues with nudity," he growled.

He kissed her again, thumbs rubbing over her nipples before his fingers moved to her bra clasp, setting her skin ablaze. His lips roamed her neck as he murmured, "Topless isn't naked, right?" His hand paused, waiting.

"No," she gasped. "I guess not." A momentary tug, and her bra fell away, breasts nestled in his warm palms. Hope pulled off her T-shirt, enjoying the way his eyes darkened as he watched her chest rise.

He eased back onto the couch, dragging her down on top of him.

Hopes Dashed?

-GRANT-

*B*reathing hard, Grant lifted his head to kiss Hope again, half afraid she'd call it off.

Dark hair fell in a delirious cloud around him, tickling his bare chest, and he coiled it into a thick rope, careful not to pull, resisting the urge to roll her over and bury himself inside her. The hell if he was going to be the next selfish prick on her list. And she was more than just a simple conquest.

Not naked. What the hell did that mean? Jeans were optional, for sure. Wearing only her panties? Not much of a barrier. He'd take care of her first, slipping his fingers beneath. Then she'd let him pull them sideways—a fun way around her decree.

She lay panting atop him, pupils dilated. Gorgeous.

Suppressing a groan, he ran his hands down her

back to her ass and ground his rock-hard cock against her.

She gave a little gasp, her fingers gripping his bare shoulder, and offered him a nipple.

He closed his lips over it, flicking it with his tongue.

Hope shrieked and rocketed up, her knee pushing off his groin, nearly crushing his balls.

Jesus. He doubled over, hands shielding his crotch.

"What happened? Are you okay?" Grant sat up, chest heaving, and adjusted his jeans.

She scrubbed madly at her ribs, breasts jiggling. "Yeah, I'm okay," she said. "Baby poked me with his cold nose. It just surprised me."

The dog wagged at his stupid name.

"Mojo, go *lie down*," Grant ordered. *Damned dog.* Had he ruined the mood? "Sorry. I should have told him in the first place. He won't bother us now." He caught her hand. "Or we could relocate." *Do not, do* not *stop, Pretty Girl.*

Hope pushed her hair back, bit her lip, and darted a glance at the clock.

"I've got time," Grant blurted out. "I'll stop if you want, but damn, I don't want to."

She retrieved her bra and shirt, and started down the hallway, long hair swaying.

Damn it.

Grant spread his hands on his thighs, fighting disappointment. *Another time.*

She glanced over her shoulder. "You coming?"

"Hell, yeah. Mojo, *stay.*" Grant leaped off the couch and followed her.

25
Twenty Percent

-HOPE-

*H*eart pounding, Hope flipped down the bedspread, peeled off her jeans, and slid her legs under the top sheet.

Grant tossed a condom onto the bedside table and scooted in behind her. One arm around her waist, he dragged her hair to the side. "Glad you didn't change your mind," he murmured against her neck, raising goosebumps. "Which side is Mojo's?"

Hope's face heated. "I, um, stopped letting him sleep on the bed. Just in case."

"Good choice." His fingers caressed her nipples. "Does this mean I can get you naked now, or do I need to work around that?" One hand drifted down her front to lightly strum across her panties and she lost her mind, craving him.

She spun around to bury her face in his perfect chest. "I'll give you a pass."

Grant swooped her onto her back and tugged

down her underwear, then his own. "Let me suit up now, so I don't have to stop." He reached for the condom.

Hope took out the rolled latex and sheathed his rampant erection, enjoying the way his eyes closed, head tipping back.

His knee nudged her thighs apart. His thumb circled over her most sensitive places, already wet, and she lifted her hips. "Not yet, Pretty Girl," he whispered.

Need built, sensations maddening, as his fingers stroked, his lips covering hers. Her heart hammered and she writhed, urging him into her, but one earth-shattering moment later, she cried out in bliss.

Grant paused, holding her close.

"Know what I call that?" he murmured. "A good start."

She laughed, limp, and Grant shifted his hips and entered her, soothing her ache.

Perfect.

His heated kisses stirred her ardor again, and his desire thrilled her. "Time for that twenty percent," he grated. "Turn around." He brought her leg up and over, rotating her onto her hands and knees. "Lower."

He gently pushed her shoulders down until her breasts brushed the sheets with every stroke.

Lower yet.

Oh, God. This angle... her most sensitive places aligned with the underside of his penis, each languid thrust exquisite.

Hope gasped. "Grant, I can't..." She'd never climaxed twice.

"You can. Trust me." Strong hands clasped her hips, his mouth roving the base of her neck as he bent low. "Or tell me to stop, and I will. But you're going to like it."

He was right.

Good God. A second orgasm crashed through her.

Afterwards, she lay pressed against him, head on his chest and shoulder. His steady breathing and slowing heartbeat lulled her to drop her guard.

Already, it was happening: his pheromones seeping into her skin, her own body's hormones fueling the rapture, contributing to the addiction, a wonderful chemical recipe bringing dreamy contentment. But biochemistry couldn't account for his dedication, kindness, and sense of humor.

I think I'm falling for him.

Oh, crap.

WEEKS SPED BY, a delicious blur of Grant, offset by duty.

Hope slumped onto the bench in the women's locker room outside the ER, after her six-to-three shift, feet and ankles aching. How could women work these hours when they were pregnant? Not that it would be an issue for her anytime soon. Maybe not ever.

Why was she even thinking about this?

But she knew. As time passed, Grant had renewed her faith that love might be possible. Real love: a two-way street. Understanding and acceptance.

Do not go there. It's an illusion. Roommates with benefits. You're both here temporarily, and he wants Baby.

Her heart clenched. Surely, he wasn't sleeping with her just to soften her up about the dog?

Was she being stupid? Since she'd first taken Grant to bed, she lost an hour every night, unable to resist the temptation. Yet instead of experiencing worse fatigue, she felt invigorated.

Too late to guard her heart.

I love him.

She changed out of scrubs and ran into Clay in the corridor.

"Hey, Hope." His easy smile flashed. "Want to get a pizza later? Joanna might come, too."

I should go. End the rotation on good terms with Clay, and Joanna had potential as a long-term friend, her prickliness finally thawing. It might be best for

Hope to spend time with someone other than Grant. But all she wanted was to go home to him. "I don't know. I'm really gassed. I might end up in the ER myself if I drive."

"Catch a nap and I'll pick you up tonight. Come on —only for a couple of hours. It'll be fun. Better than sitting at home."

"Okay." Grant had encouraged her to get out. Besides, it wouldn't hurt for her stalker to see other people stopping by to check on her, if he really was watching.

"Awesome. Where do you live?"

She gave Clay her address, drove home, and went straight to bed after playing with Baby.

It seemed like only moments passed before the doorbell rang. Hope stumbled over and looked through the peephole, revealing a fish-eye view of Clayton P. Rothrock, III, in tan chinos and a blue button-down with rolled-up sleeves.

She opened the door. "Hi, Clay. Come on in while I wash my face and change into jeans."

He sat on the couch, glancing around, but he spooked when the pet door burst open and Baby rushed over.

Hope said, "It's okay. He's friendly." Well, not exactly *friendly*, but not aggressive.

"I'll say." Clay leaned back while Baby sniffed him

thoroughly, from feet to shoulders and back to hands.

The dog sat, eyes fixed on Hope. Completely still —not even a wag.

That's funny. She wouldn't have figured Baby would take to Clay, of all people, though she couldn't have said why, exactly. Maybe it was a good sign, though, that the dog was finally mellowing towards people besides her and Grant. "I'll be right out," she said, and went to change.

Baby was in the same spot when she came out. He stared at her. Was he hoping she'd stay in?

"Sorry, Baby, but I'll be back. Good boy."

Hope texted Grant and left with Clay, feeling guilty about the dog's whine.

26
Find Sit

-GRANT-

*G*rant frowned when he got Hope's text, two hours before his shift ended: **Out to dinner with friends. See you later.**

He'd looked forward to seeing her all day. Sparring with her was such fun, and she "got" it, his need to protect and save—she was the same way.

No. It's good she's getting out. She works way too hard.

And he could use the time to plan some things. He imagined taking off with Hope and Mojo through the mountains.

That was a great idea; she was almost done with her rotation here. *I'll set something up and tell her how I feel. See if she'll give us a shot.*

Have fun, he texted.

The snowmobile and ATV vendors watched the thinning traffic like vultures assessing a pulse, some already packing up.

Overdue for his break, Grant headed for the food tent.

A British accent made him glance over—and look again. He'd recognize those cheekbones and red buzzcut anywhere—it was Smith, the lead guitarist with the Whiskey Barrels! He sat joking with his bandmates—and the cute girl Grant had rescued—over plates of barbecue.

Hell, yeah! Their CD was still in his glovebox—it had felt like too soon to give it to Hope right after he'd razzed her about her beloved older Jeep's sound system. *"Good for road trips,"* she'd said, her tone wistful.

Grant turned and ran to his pickup.

He dug it out and rushed back, afraid he'd miss them, but they were still there. He slowed and breathed deep, then sauntered closer.

"Officer Calloway!" sang the girl with a smile—the perfect opening.

"Hey," he said, nonchalant. "Surprised to see you back."

The girl beamed up at her boyfriend. "Derrick's looking for a place here."

"Cool." Grant fumbled the disc and a fine-tipped marker out of his cargo pocket. "Hey, my girlfriend loves you guys but had to miss your show. Would you mind signing it?"

"You got it, mate," said the guitarist, Rupert. He plucked the disc out of Grant's hand, slit the shrink wrap, and slid out the cover booklet with the lyrics. "What's her name?"

"Hope. Hope Hernandez."

"Awesome," said West.

The band gathered around, each scribbling something on the insert.

"She'll love you forever, man." The singer handed it back.

Grant's heart ached, just a little bit, as he pocketed the CD. "Thanks, gentlemen."

Forever sounds pretty damned good.

AT THE END of his shift, he drove home, thinking. He didn't like the touristy nature of Bear Creek, but the Rockies made up for that: gorgeous, with the promise of year-round adventure. He could definitely make it work, if Hope was willing to give it a try.

I'll plan a romantic getaway. Maybe rent a cabin in the mountains and give her the CD then.

Mojo danced and whirled when Grant stepped into the house, but it seemed quiet without Hope. After he played with Mojo, fed him, and walked him,

Grant microwaved some soup and booted up his laptop.

"Time to find another gig, Mojo. If I have something better lined up here, it'll show her I'm taking this seriously."

Should he wait to see if she got the position?

Grant shook his head. "You know how smart she is, and how driven—that woman is savage," he told Mojo. "No way will they turn her down."

There were regional search and rescue teams, and Mojo would be a natural for that, once Hope recognized that a working dog needed an outlet to thrive. A nose like his could help find avalanche victims, lost hikers and skiers, or even crashed airplanes. It'd be another way to be a hero, this time without the risk of turning into pink mist.

Grant mapped out every decent job within an hours' commute—she'd want to live here in town, close to the ER—and spent three hours submitting applications. He'd surprise her once she got the official notice from Bear Creek Medical.

It was nearly eleven when Mojo sat up, wagging.

Grant crossed the room, opened the door, and Hope greeted him with a kiss. It felt like slipping into faded jeans and bare feet, after a day in slacks and dress shoes.

"Hey, Pretty Girl. Did you have fun with your

buddies? I guess they're not exactly *buddies,* though, if you're competing for the same position." He followed her to the couch.

"Oh? Are we not buddies, even though we both want Baby?" Her smile warmed him.

"We are. I'm just really liking this joint custody."

A little crease formed between her eyebrows. Was she worried about him leaving soon?

But all she said was, "Yeah, it was nice. And guess what? Baby loved Clay. Parked right next to him until we left." She smiled. "It's good to see him getting used to civilian life."

"That doesn't sound like Mojo." Not only was he aloof to strangers, but he usually had good instincts, and though Hope had never said anything negative about him, this Clay sounded like a jackass.

Hope bent to shake the dog's ruff. "Yeah, walked up, sniffing and wagging, plunked down, and stayed there. Baby looked at me like he was daring me to send him away."

Shit. That sounded a lot like a Find Sit. But an ER doc, making bombs? *That's crazy. Narcotics? Surely not enough to—*

Jesus. Had Mojo caught a whiff of magazine cologne samples from Clay? He *was* her rival.

Am I overreacting? Better be sure, instead of

accusing a guy he'd never met. It'd been weeks since Mojo learned the scent.

If I could just see his reaction...

Grant forced a smile. "That's great." His mind raced—how to orchestrate another meeting? "We should have him over this weekend. The other resident, too, and anyone else you work with. A casual end-of-tour thing."

Hope shot a glance at him and her lips curved.

Did she think Grant was staking a claim? Or did she like the idea of them as a unit? Either was fine with him.

She looked around the little house and sighed. "I guess we could order pizza."

"Come on, Pretty Girl. It'll be fun." Of course, she'd be too exhausted to want to cook on her day off. "You won't have to do a thing. I'll grill burgers."

And grill this guy Clay, if I need to.

Hope gave a cautious smile and it felt like he'd won the lottery. "Thanks, Grant. I'm glad you have my back."

Oh, Pretty Girl, you have no idea.

A Time to Grill

-GRANT-

*T*he next day, Grant arranged to rent a little mountain chalet near a lake. A killer view, a king-size bed, and a hot tub overlooking the valley below.

A perfect spot for him to persuade Hope to keep *him*, in addition to the dog.

Time to tell her how I feel.

If she got the ER job here, he'd deal with the touristy nature of Bear Creek.

Grant made arrangements for the cookout, grimly eager to evaluate her colleagues. When the day finally arrived, he took down the ziplock of glued-up letters. How soon to cue Mojo in?

While she gets dressed. That would be an hour or so before folks arrived.

Grant paced, keyed up. He'd keep it quiet, but if Mojo got no hits, Grant could tell Hope, and that would give her some peace of mind, at least, that it was none of her colleagues.

Mojo leaped up and rushed to stare through the living room window, tail wagging, thrilled that Hope was home.

Me, too, buddy. Grant settled for pouring her a cup of coffee. "Hey, Pretty Girl."

Her tired eyes lit up with a smile as she accepted it. "Thanks." She took a sip, set it on the countertop, and leaned against him, sighing.

He put his arms around her, as if he could take on some of her fatigue, and she laid her head on his shoulder.

After a moment, she pushed away. "I'd better shower and get things ready."

"Got it covered. Already vacuumed and made the patties. Just put your feet up."

"Really? My hero." She kissed him and headed down the hall.

Grant opened the ziplock and held it out to Mojo. *"Find."*

His partner thoroughly sniffed the contents, wagged, and started around the perimeter.

When the doorbell rang, Grant opened the door to a tall, smiling blonde.

"Hi, I'm Joanna Sutters."

"Good to meet you. Come through to the back;

Hope'll be right out. This is Mojo—er, Baby," Grant amended, when she frowned.

"Hi, Baby!" Joanna knelt, cooing.

Wagging, he snuffled her, toes to hair, and resumed his patrol, a freakin' pushbutton.

Pride in his dog swelled Grant's chest. He asked Joanna, "What are you drinking?"

Grant got her a Dos Equis and greeted the other guests. Mainly ER staff—a desk clerk, staff nurses and physicians, an infection specialist, a couple of surgeons, but not this Clay character.

Hope and Mojo made the rounds. She laughed with their guests, while Grant fiddled with the grill, watching his dog carefully.

Maybe it was all for nothing. Mojo would be getting tired of this, too, distracted by the smell of the burgers. It was a stupid idea. Crazy.

Out front, a BMW parked at the curb. A young guy wearing blue scrubs sauntered toward the front door.

Grant returned his attention to the Chinese doc's joke.

"... vowed she'd do her own stitches, so I said, 'suture self.'"

"Clay!" Hope's greeting made Grant look up as the guy in scrubs came through into the yard, his slick, styled hair straight out of GQ.

Grant prompted Mojo for another round. *"Find."*

The dog headed for Hope and the new arrival, sniffed him, and sat, stock-still.

Shit. You son of a bitch.

Clay petted Mojo and smiled at Hope.

Grant unclenched his hands and busied himself with laying down another row of burgers and brats on the grill. Smoke rose, fragrant, yet his stomach soured.

He had to make sure—and then what? Hope was so worried about upsetting the hospital, and the notes weren't quite criminal. And she was too kind, too forgiving.

He strolled over to his woman and the jackass, and stuck out his hand. "Grant Calloway. What are you drinking?"

"Clay Rothrock." Cool blue eyes appraised him, though the guy smiled. "Beer'll do." He paused. "Oh, hey, I brought dip. It's in my backpack." He glanced at the house.

Grant reached into the cooler, opened a bottle, and handed it to the man, instead of using it to crush his windpipe. "I'll grab it—I'm going in anyway."

"I'll go, too," Clay said.

To keep me away?

Reasonable, though, to prevent people from

digging through his backpack. "Come on, Mojo. Let's go *find* it."

The dog loped beside Grant as he crossed to the back porch with Clay. The screen door banged.

Mojo made a circuit of the room, nosed eagerly at a green backpack at the end of the couch, and sat.

You sleazy son of a bitch.

Grant wrestled down a surge of anger. Cold logic was the key here.

Unlikely Clay would be carrying a cut-up magazine or glue around. Would scissors be circumstantial evidence, at least? The motherlode would be an actual letter. A long shot, though one of them had been dropped off instead of mailed. Would he try to leave one today, scheming to get Hope rattled in front of everyone?

Clay laughed as he walked over. "Smart dog. It's like he can smell it. I thought his name was Baby, though?" His smug smile implied that Grant was out of the loop.

"Yeah. *Baby* can smell odors at a concentration of one part per billion. He's never had a false alarm."

How can I legally get that backpack open? And get Hope away for a bit? Grant had to be careful not to botch this or her job prospects.

"Handy for sniffing out junk food." Clay brought out a tub of bean dip and zipped the pack.

"Other things, too," Grant said, watching him carefully. "Will you take it out to Hope? I'll be right there. I gotta grab the chips."

"Uh..." Clay glanced at Mojo, then shrugged. "Sure." He carried the dip out the screen door.

"Good boy, Mojo." Ignoring the temptation to dive for the pack, Grant raced to the little pantry, set the opened chip bag on the floor, and bumped a case of beer over onto it. He scooped up the crushed package. "Mojo. *Guard.*"

Grant strode outside, leaving his dog beside the backpack.

Smoke rose from the grill. *Shit, I burned the brats.*

Grant tossed the bag to Hope as he passed. "I smashed the chips. Let me flip the meat and I'll go get more."

"Geez, Grant. What did you do?" She laughed, peering into the bag. "They're pulverized."

"Knocked over a case of beer. Give me a minute and I'll head out." He turned the burgers over and adjusted the sizzling brats—one a lost cause, but Mojo had earned it.

Hope laughed. "I'll do it. Better that than manning the grill. Want to come, Joanna?"

Off they went, chatting.

Good.

Clay ambled to the house, about-faced, and marched up to Grant. "Hey, man, that dog's sitting next to my backpack, growling. I need something out of it."

So do I, asshole.

Grant lifted his chin at the nearby ER nurse. "Say, mind watching these for a minute?" He handed over the spatula. "Thanks."

"What's the deal with him?" Clay asked as they turned toward the house. "Hope said he was an explosives dog, but I'm no bomber."

"Funny you should ask," Grant said. "He's trained to detect other things, too: drugs, guns, contraband, anything I want."

They walked through the back door.

Clay stopped at Mojo's low growl. "Shit!"

"Yep." Grant closed the door behind them. "Sometimes people do, when he hits them. He won't do that, though—unless I tell him to."

"I need my backpack, man. I ... just got a page and have to go."

"Problem is, he's found the scent I was after," Grant said. "The one that matches the letters Hope got."

Clay's eyes widened and he darted a glance at Mojo, who rumbled, hackles standing on end. "What?" He attempted a nonchalant laugh, but his voice went up an octave. "What are you talking about?"

"You know, so cut the shit."

Clay drew himself up, blustering. "I don't know what—"

"Mojo, show us those *pearly whites.*"

The growl grew louder. Mojo's lips drew back from impressive teeth.

The bastard paled. "Look, there's been a mistake."

"I'll say," Grant said. "In the field, this is where we'd usually draw our weapons. See if the perps are as smart as they think. But here, calling the police is the quickest way to straighten this all out. Your training program would hear about it, too, of course. Do you see any other option?"

"I never meant it. It was a joke—"

"Bullshit. You're afraid she's better than you, so you tried to scare her away with those chickenshit anonymous letters."

"It won't happen again, I swear." Clay spread his hands.

"No. It won't. Not here, not ever. You need to walk out now, withdraw your application, and keep walking."

"Okay. Please... just don't contact my program director." Clay glanced again at Mojo.

Behind him, people chatted in the backyard,

oblivious, but Hope would be back soon, so Grant had to hurry. For now, what she didn't know wouldn't hurt her. Once it was completely over, he'd tell her.

He pulled out his phone. "First, we'll do a photo shoot, starting with you with your hands up next to my dog, and then whatever's in your backpack, asshole. Then you can go."

Grant clicked a photo.

At the point of no return, Clay's jaw tightened.

"Or I call the cops right now. Your choice." If the bastard called his bluff, Hope would be pissed that he'd collared Clay, and possibly involved the hospital. *She'll get over it.*

"Okay! Just get him off me."

Mojo was just sitting there but Grant couldn't blame Clay for not wanting to reach past those dripping fangs.

"All done. Come."

The dog bounded to him and Clay lunged, sweeping up his backpack. His eyes darted to the door.

"Don't even think about it. He's faster than you. What's in the backpack?"

Clay pressed his lips together and jerked open his pack. He pulled out an envelope, just like the others.

Bingo.

Grant snapped a photo. "Open it and hold it up.... Good."

The message came into focus:

WHAT'S UNDER THOSE SCRUBS?

It took everything Grant had not to throttle the bastard. "Put it on the coffee table."

The son of a bitch complied while Grant documented it.

"Okay. Don't ever pull this shit again. My military network means I have friends all over, and some of them are freakin' ninjas. I'll be watching. Every triumph she has, every heartbreak, will remind me to follow up. If you step out of line, I'll send this to your boss, the police, your hometown paper, your mother, and your freakin' country club, then I'll personally come pay you a visit—with Mojo—and it sure as hell won't be anonymous."

"Fine. I got it." Clay blotted sweat from his forehead. "Can I go now?"

From the corner of his eye, Grant saw Hope's Jeep pull up.

"Beat it."

The bastard rushed out the front door.

Grant grabbed a plastic grocery bag. Using it like a mitten, he scooped up the letter and inverted the sack over it as Hope and Joanna walked in with a couple bags of chips.

"Where's Clay off to? He didn't look so good—is he sick?" Hope frowned.

"Yeah, he is." That was true enough.

Grant kissed her. "Thanks for getting the chips."

28
Shattered

-HOPE-

*C*linging to dreams, Hope snuggled into the cozy spot Grant vacated early the next morning.

"Just sleep," he whispered. Warm lips brushed her forehead. The mattress shifted and the doorknob rattled as his voice drifted back. "I love you, Pretty Girl."

Elation jolted her awake despite her sleep deprivation. She sat up, heart thumping, but his pickup rumbled, and he was gone.

It wasn't a dream.

She hopped up and hugged her dog. "Did you hear that, Baby? He loves me!" She bounced in to shower, her fatigue briefly forgotten.

When Hope arrived in the ER, Joanna asked, "Did you hear about Clay? He had to leave for a family emergency. He's not coming back."

"Wow, that's awful. I hope things will be okay."

It must be something dire, for him to leave with two days left in the rotation. Crunch time, when a program would decide whether or not to make an offer. Was that why he'd looked so shaken?

Hope texted: **Sorry to hear you have a family emergency. Let me know if I can help.**

He never answered.

Raymond Koonce called her into his office at three.

"We've been impressed with your work—and that's saying a lot, alongside Dr. Rothrock."

She suppressed irritation that Clay was the yardstick by which she was measured—he was a good doc, if a little slick. Hope waited for the CEO to come to the point.

"Dr. Rothrock's withdrawn his application—a family emergency, you understand," Koonce hastened to add, as if to make it clear that, of course, anyone would kill to work at Bear Creek Medical. "We'd like to offer you the position." He beamed.

Hope's smile broke out before she tamed it to an expression more appropriate for Clay's misfortune.

Koonce didn't seem to notice, waxing poetic about the institution. "...We're confident you'll uphold our high standards," and her mind flashed to Grant's earlier comments about Koonce brushing off the letters: *"You don't think that's a bad sign? You'd work at a place like that? You could get a job anywhere."*

The CEO concluded, "We'll send a contract in the next couple of days."

Her father's words surfaced in her mind: *"Hope is a powerful force, because it harnesses time. It encompasses optimism, and the patience to wait for the right opportunity, and to put in the work. Hope means not settling."*

It *wasn't* good that Koonce had expected her to ignore the risk to her safety to avoid bad press. But she liked most of the people she worked with...

Hope stalled, so tired she was afraid she'd say the wrong thing.

"Thank you. I'll watch for it."

She went back to work, staying three hours extra because of a cluster of food poisoning cases, both staff and patients. She made a mental note to *never* eat at Lickety Split Chicken.

Hope finally trudged home, yawning.

Baby danced around her, wagging as if she hadn't broken her promise to walk him. "I'm sorry I'm late."

Guilt tugged at her for not holding up her end. The truth was, if not for Grant, the dog would be one sad pup, left alone so much. But she'd dragged her feet setting up a pet sitter, unwilling to think about how bleak it would be when Grant left.

"I guess it's good we do have Grant, huh, Baby?"

She straightened, hearing his voice drifting from the back porch. Hope shrugged off her white coat and slung it over the wooden kitchen chair. She went to the fridge for iced tea, noting the new bag of dog food in the pantry. She hadn't even registered it was running low.

Baby deserved better. Was she always doomed to fall short?

I'll see if Grant wants a drink. She filled two glasses with ice. When Hope closed the freezer, she caught his phone call.

"—yet. I'm not leaving without Mojo."

Leaving? She'd hoped they'd have some time together, now that she was finally done, to explore the region and the possibility for a relationship that could last. Hope paused, peering out the open window.

Grant slouched on the swing, the top of his head visible. "Not really. I don't like the town."

A tendril of anxiety crept into her. She'd thought ... Hope swallowed and listened harder, feeling crummy for eavesdropping but doing it anyway.

"I know. I promised, didn't I? That still gives me a few days—"

Days?

"—to work on her—"

Oh, God. What did that mean?

"—before I get back to Broken Arrow."

Crap—he's really leaving? Her chest squeezed. *He said he loved me.*

Had he changed his mind, and was just staying for Baby?

"—I'm here for my dog, whatever it takes."

"I love you," he'd said. Was it only a scheme so she'd lower her guard and he could get Baby?

No. That can't be true.

She'd talk to Grant. *Later. I'm too fried now to have a heavy-duty talk.*

Hope took a swallow of tea to dilute the acid in her stomach and stepped onto the porch. She raised the glass, inquiring.

He shook his head and hung up.

Baby pranced over to her with his ball, wagging.

"Hey, Pretty Girl." Grant scooted over, watching her toss the ball for Baby. "He's a happy dog." Not a word of reproach, no snide comments that it was about time she played with him. He'd stopped pointing out that Baby was better off with him—was it because it was so obvious?

Baby ran over to Grant with the ball and Hope's chest constricted. If he was leaving, what was the right thing to do for her dog?

"All done." He draped one arm over her shoulders. Baby flopped down, almost on Grant's feet, gazing up at him. "I booked a cabin in the mountains for us, for

the weekend, to celebrate your finishing up. I thought it'd be nice for you, since you haven't been able to get out much—"

Was this part of his "working on her" plan?

"—and I promised to give Tony's law firm a try."

"You're leaving?" Her heart turned over.

"I'm not sure," he said. "'A try' doesn't mean long term, and I do like it here."

But he told his brother he didn't.

How could Grant lie so easily? And if he lied about enjoying Bear Creek, what others had he told?

"Oh." Hope bit her lip, at a loss. "They offered me the job," she said, wishing she felt more excited. "Clay withdrew from consideration."

For a split second, smug satisfaction flitted across Grant's face. "Congratulations. That's terrific."

He's not surprised.

Hope stared at him. "You *knew?*" She shook her head. "How could you know that? I haven't told anyone."

He raked his hand through his hair, staring across the lawn, then faced her. "Clay was your pen pal. Mojo sniffed him out."

"What? *Clay* sent the letters?" *That lying weasel!* "Why didn't you tell me?" Hope frowned. *Oh, shit—* Clay's sudden departure that day. "Grant, what did you do?"

His jaw tightened. "Took pictures. Told him to leave town or I'd turn him in." He raised his hands. "He had no idea I was bluffing, but this way you're completely clean. It kept you from having to make the call or letting him off easy."

"Leaving town *is* easy, after all that. It wasn't your call to make!"

"He won't be pulling that shit again. I made sure of that, and—"

"So, you *threatened* him?"

"It wasn't a threat."

"You'd have hurt him?" Hope gaped at him. Did she really know him at all? "What did you say?"

Grant's nostrils flared. "Told the bastard I knew people and would be checking up on him—and I will, to keep him honest."

"Honest? *You* can say that? Were you ever going to tell me?"

"I had to make a decision. You were the one who wanted to avoid the police—"

"Because of that damned job! The one I got after *you* ran off my competition!"

He frowned, shrugging. "Come on, Hope, be reasonable. You don't know that's why you got the gig."

He didn't think she was the best candidate? Fury hit her, a brick to the chest.

Did she get the offer only because Clay left?

Grant wasn't done. "And does it really matter? He was an undeserving prick. Now he's gone, you've lost your stalker, and gotten your dream job—"

"Through unfair tactics!"

His eyes flashed. "A little hypocritical, aren't you? You, who took my best friend because some two-star rolled through and pressured the staff?"

Hope gasped, recalling her father's casual words, when she'd told him she might adopt: *"Mmm. This is the outfit at Lackland?"* How quick they'd been to process the adoption.

She shook her head, rejecting it even as the truth settled heavy in her gut, nauseating. No wonder Grant thought she'd stolen Baby—and would do whatever he had to, to get him back.

How could Dad have done that? He was as bad as Grant—both willing to puppeteer behind the scenes, while claiming they valued her independence. Cheapening her victories, when she'd tried so hard to make her way on merit, not sex or race or connections.

Grant crossed his arms, frowning as if he were the one wronged.

Hurt and anger boiled in her veins at the double betrayal. The crazy urge to backhand him was almost overwhelming—and frightening. She clasped trembling fingers together. A man who tempted her to violence—what was she thinking? That it could all work out, so they could be a happy family? No wonder it seemed too good to be true.

Deep down, she'd known better.

Hope took a quick breath, got up, and trudged into the kitchen.

Grant followed her, hands clenched on the back of the barstool.

From the corner of her eye, the new green bag of kibble gleamed, a shiny testament to her failure. Mocking her impending loss.

Tears blurred the label on the bag, but she was still Hope-Will-Do-It Hernandez.

It was the right thing for Baby.

She swallowed, turned, and knelt.

"Mojo, *come.*"

Grant's head whipped around but the dog wagged and pranced over to her, happy regardless of which name she chose.

Hope hugged him, burying her face in his warm fur as a knife twisted in her throat. "You're a good boy," she whispered.

She raised her face to Grant. "I'm going for a drive. Take whatever you need for him, but I want you out of my house by the time I get back. Leave the key in the mailbox."

His eyes widened. "Hope, no—"

"You don't get to make this call," she snapped, standing. He'd managed her. Manipulated her. It had to stop. "I can't trust you—and vice versa, apparently —you think I'm someone underhanded! You got what you came for, and more. Just call it a win and get out."

"You're dumping me, just like that? I can't believe this—"

"Believe it."

Grant threw his hands up. "That's it? No more joint custody? We're done and you're giving me Mojo?"

"Yes. Not that you deserve him—you don't. But you're the best person for him right now—and I'll never forgive you for that."

Hope spun, jerked a T-shirt from her call bag, and flung it at Grant. "Give him this to remember me by."

"Hope, wait. Hope—"

Angry tears brimming, she stormed out of the house.

29
Too Late ?

-GRANT-

*J*esus. Grant felt like throwing up. Hope's T-shirt hung limply from his hand.

Mojo whined, wagging uncertainly.

"Can you believe that shit?" Grant demanded. "What the hell was I supposed to do? She'd have been so pissed if I'd called the cops. If I'd let him walk, we'd have never had the chance to nail him again. But she'd have caved and let him off."

He appealed to Mojo. "Since when is it a crime to protect the woman you love?"

Mojo broke eye contact, ears drooping.

Grant leaped up, pacing. "What am I going to do now? She won't listen."

He didn't dare push her, not after all the shit with the stalker. "Goddammit. That's what I get for telling her the whole thing."

He held hard to his anger, to keep sadness away.

Maybe he should have mentioned the cabin

215

earlier. Built it up. Women loved that romantic shit. Maybe she'd have been mellower.

Shouldn't have called her out about the two-star. Of course, she'd be embarrassed.

He flung himself down on the couch and stared up at the ceiling. "Should have told her, I guess. Should've known I couldn't just quietly take care of it."

He sighed. "Looks like we're leaving, Mojo. Her house, her rules. Good thing I booked the goddamned cabin."

Mojo whined again, picking up on Grant's turmoil.

"Sorry, buddy. Didn't mean to get us thrown out of the pack."

He stood and went into the bedroom to stuff his belongings into a duffle. "She won't want me to stalk her, and I'll be damned if I'm going to grovel."

He shoved the last of his clothes into his bag and hesitated, the CD in his hand. He scribbled a note on the back of a pizza flyer instead of a nice card—*real charming, Calloway*—and left it on the table with the disc.

"We'll check out that cabin and give it a few days. She'll come around."

Won't she?

Scorched Earth

-HOPE-

*G*rant's pickup was gone when Hope returned to the duplex. She trudged up the steps.

Empty. Just as she'd demanded.

The old familiar loneliness slammed into her chest like 300 joules. She caught her breath and shoved the pain down hard.

It's good he's gone. She didn't need the temptation of a normal life—that was still out of reach.

And Baby—Mojo... He'll be happy. He doesn't know what a jerk Grant is.

He'd left her something. She picked up a Whiskey Barrels CD—minus the shrink wrap—and a scrawled note—**I'm sorry. Please come**—with a scribbled address.

Had she made a mistake? The grief packed tighter, a black hole that threatened to swallow her.

Hope fed her anger into it. A guy who made decisions for her...where would that end? And what a crappy, two-word apology, written on a pizza flyer! He'd probably found the CD at his job or dug it out of a trash bin.

Even now, she wasn't worth the effort.

Mail dropped into the box, and she stomped out to get it. At least there'd be no more creepy letters. One was from Bear Creek Medical—an end-of-rotation survey? But no—it was a crisp, formal job offer, signed with a flourish by Raymond Koonce.

Hope's jaw clenched at the memory of his slick, patronizing certainty that their reputation was more important than her safety. The sudden urge to drive over and throw it in his face seized her. Afterwards, she'd stop by that cabin and rip Grant apart before driving fifteen hours to rail at her dad. And then she'd write Clay's residency program and the state medical board to nuke his future. He'd pay for those weeks of fear.

Get a grip. One thing at a time. She took a deep breath, but they *still* all sounded good. "Shit!" Tears stung her eyes, but there was no one to listen to her outburst, no adoring eyes and slow wag. She'd sent away her only real friend.

Hope took another calming breath. She was trained to handle anything. She'd get through this, too.

Grant's text made her phone vibrate.

I can't deal with it now. What good would talking do? He hadn't denied any of it at the time.

One thing at a time. She'd start with the fifteen-hour drive.

I've had enough of Bear Creek.

31
Fading Hopes
-GRANT-

*G*rant and Mojo pulled up to the little log cabin as the sunset tinted its spectacular mountain backdrop pink. A wide porch with rocking chairs, a split rail fence.

He carried in groceries, wine, and the red roses he'd bought, just in case. Inside, it was cozy: a rustic fireplace, polished flagstone, a braided rug—she'd love it.

Grant checked his phone—nothing. "She'll come," he told Mojo, but his chest twinged with each breath.

Evening became night, and they spent it alone, Grant penning heartfelt apologies on the cards he'd bought.

In the morning, he sent a text: **I'm here, and I'm so sorry. Please come.**

No reply.

He drove into town and knocked on Hope's door.

When she didn't answer, he dropped one of the cards into the mail slot.

Grant and Mojo took short hikes, afraid to be gone too long, and the sunlight on snowy peaks eased the tightness in his chest. *She'll come. She's got the job here.*

"She loves *you,* at least," he told Mojo. "Ironic after tracking her down to get you, now you're the key to getting her back."

His phone call that afternoon went to voice-mail. Grant swallowed and tried not to sound desperate. "Hey, Hope. Look, I'm really sorry. I'm still here but ... if you don't want to come, please call me. I—"

The beep cut him off before he could get too pathetic.

Mojo looked at him and whined.

"She'll come, buddy." Grant rested his forehead in his palms. "But I sure wish *you* could call her."

Over the next two days, the roses drooped and withered, fallen crimson petals fading.

Grant tried again the night before he left, but she wasn't home. He dropped off the last card, scrawling, **I'll stay until five p.m. Sunday**.

Twenty minutes before Grant had to turn in the key on the last day, he shoved his clothes into a bag while Mojo whined.

The wilted roses made his chest ache. Was it really over?

He threw the flowers in the trash and dumped the water.

"I'm sorry, too, buddy, but I can't make her forgive me." He forced a smile, as if it were actually possible to bullshit the dog. "We'll head back to Broken Arrow and test drive the life of a lawyer. All those skunks."

He sighed. "Four-legged ones, too. And possums. You'll love it." At least Mojo wouldn't miss the majestic scenery and mountain air.

Ten hours to Tulsa. The mountains receded, the heat grew, and every damned station was playing The Whiskey Barrels' latest.

At first, Grant stabbed the radio off—the band couldn't be that great, if Hope was unmoved by his CD, but with time, curiosity overcame the monotony of the road and his glum spirits.

The next time he heard, "And here's The Whiskey Barrels' barn-burner hit, 'Kondo K.O.,'" he let it play, the jaunty chords at odds with the sappy lyrics:

> *I just thought I'd make the offer*
> *Since it wasn't ever used*
> *Ain't no big deal that you don't want it*
> *And no surprise it was refused*

Grant swallowed, the air in his lungs dry from the AC.

> *I forgot I even had one*
> *Pointless, far as I could see*
> *Neglected, veiled in dust and cobwebs*
> *Since it never "sparked joy" in me*

Grant snorted. How had they made millions with this shit? The lyrics were just like astrology—they could be twisted to fit any situation.

> *Ain't no big deal that you don't want it*
> *I just thought I'd try, at least*
> *Didn't mean to make you stumble*
> *When I laid it at your feet*

His own chest twinged, and he rested a hand on his dog. "She'll be okay, buddy, since that asshole's gone. She doesn't need us anymore."

> *It felt really good to give*
> *To find a home for it at last*
> *Light, uncluttered, more alive*

*But one man's treasure is someone else's
trash*

Grant gripped the wheel, eyes straight ahead, unaffected.

Bourbon'll do just fine to numb—

Grant snapped off the radio. "This is why I don't like country," he told Mojo.

Would Hope think of them when she heard that damned song?

She'd be missing Mojo—she loved *him*, if not Grant.

"It's not like with us, though," he told the dog. "She only knew you for a few months." But that didn't stop him from feeling shitty as he rolled toward the flatlands. "The song's got one thing right, anyway: Bourbon's not a bad idea."

32
Confrontation

-HOPE-

*E*ars ringing from sleep deprivation, jangling nerves egged on by Mountain Dew, Hope braked in front of her parents' house and marched up to the door.

Her dad opened it. *"Mijita!"* He folded her into a hug, as she stood stiffly.

Nuke whirled and pranced around them.

Her father pulled back with a frown.

Mom joined them, exclaiming, "What's wrong, sweetheart?"

"You pulled strings to get me that dog?"

His eyes widened, while her mother's narrowed.

Dad spread his hands. "I just went to check out the facility and pay a visit to Colonel Westmoreland," he protested. "I only—"

"You went in person?" Hope glared. "No wonder the soldier thought I stole Baby! He tracked me down in Colorado!"

"He did?" Dad's shocked expression gave way to thunderclouds. "What's his name?"

"Stop. He's medically *retired,* Dad. You can't touch him. Even if you could, it's not your place to interfere."

"Interfere?" His eyebrows went up. "Just because I want to make sure my daughter—"

"Enrique." A single word from her mom was all it took to quell him. She looked closely at Hope, then told him, "Why don't you wait for us inside?" Before he could answer, she herded him through the door and shut it, then gestured to the porch swing.

Hope sat, joined by her mother.

"What's this all about, sweetheart?" Mom's arm came around her.

Hope spilled out the whole story, concluding, "So it was my dream job but I just can't work there now. And Grant..." She swallowed. "I was so angry. But now... I love him, Mom. I still do."

Her mother squeezed her, not a single I-told-you-so forthcoming. "It was so much at once, sounds like: betrayed by your colleague, the hospital administration threw you under the bus, your dad's meddling, and losing Baby and Grant, and you've been working like—well, a dog. Maybe just sleep on it? Then you can allocate your anger according to blame, rather than crush everyone under its combined weight."

Hope laughed, her frustration easing. "That makes sense. But Clay can go to hell, and so can Koonce and Bear Creek."

"Okay, that's three down. Let the others percolate a bit?"

But how long would Grant wait? Regret squeezed her heart as she remembered his bewildered, hurt expression. "It might already be too late."

Mom chuckled. "That dog will love you forever, and men are much the same."

Hope's eyes stung. Could that be true?

Her mother smiled. "One other similarity is that they can both be trained, *if* they know what you want. Men are creatures of action, who want to protect. They don't dither, they *decide,* then execute that plan, and sometimes that means mistakes. Not even a stellar man—or dog—can read your mind."

She hugged Hope again. "Go talk to your father, sweetheart. He'll be feeling terrible. Maybe Grant does, too."

Hope breathed deep and slipped into the house.

Her dad rose as she entered, his face drawn. *"Mijita,* I'm sorry. I only meant to help." He rubbed his forehead. "What can I do to fix it?"

"Nothing. Not a thing. It's my issue, just like the job." Hope slumped into the kitchen chair.

"They'll want you anywhere you apply."

"Maybe, but I don't want just any job—I want to have a life. Be able to get out and do things." *Keep a relationship alive.* She sighed. "I'm thinking about doing locum tenens work. I could work weekends only, or two weeks a month, and maybe travel. There's this company called AlphaMed that sounds interesting. They work with a lot of ex-military and the woman who runs it liked that I was raised Army, though she was Navy."

"A woman, huh? And a squid?" Her dad frowned. "Senator Larssen mentioned something... What's her name? I'll bet I know—"

"No, Dad. You've got to *stop.*"

He looked so crestfallen that she hurried on. "I'm grateful for your support, but I need to do it on my own, unless I ask you for help. This is the new normal —it has to be."

His lips compressed, then he nodded. "Only if you ask." He grinned and hugged her tight. "But if you do, I'll move heaven and earth."

Hope waited two days, then wrote to Clay's residency program in Georgia and the state medical board. She was not about to let him get away with his scheme unscathed, nor depend on Grant's threat to keep the jerk in line. How many similar things had Clay done, to hamstring his competition? The allegations would follow him for years.

He should have thought of that.

Once that was done, she applied to AlphaMed and wrote a letter to the CEO and board at Bear Creek Medical.

Dear Mr. Koonce,

   I must decline your offer of a position at Bear Creek Medical Center. Though it was my fondest wish when I started there, I cannot bring myself to work at a facility that puts their reputation above their worker's safety...

Let Koonce explain that to the board.

There would be other worthwhile places in Colorado.

The only things left on her list were Baby and Grant. A giant hollow cored out of her soul, yet she'd ignored his calls and texts. She scrolled through them, kicking herself. Was it too late?

Hope pulled out the CD, studying the cover, and slid out the insert to look at the lyrics while she thought about how to approach him.

Oh, my God. It's signed by the band. That's why the shrink-wrap was gone. How had he managed that?

On the last page, Grant had written, **All my love, Pretty Girl.**

Love.

Eyes brimming, Hope traced her finger over the line, remembering her mom's words: *"They don't dither, they decide, then execute that plan, and sometimes that means mistakes."*

She was more like Grant than she realized.

Hope picked up her phone and tapped out, **How's my dog?**

No. Too easy to ignore a text. Her only chance was to try to make amends in person.

The truth was she couldn't stand to be away from him a minute longer. She erased it and googled law firms in Broken Arrow.

Time to take a road trip.

33
Dyed in the Wool

-GRANT-

week into his sentence, Grant loosened his tie and pulled off the suit coat as the Tulsa breeze hit him like a blow dryer on high. Already sweating, he laid the garment on the blistering seat of his pickup and cranked the AC. The weather was one more damned thing he missed about Colorado.

Hope was out there somewhere, saving lives, while he stayed with Tony, stuck doing research at his brother's law firm.

He sighed. Why did Tony want to talk to him tonight?

Grant had tried—he'd really tried—but it was clear he wasn't cut out for lawyering. His attention wandered, though to be fair, it was probably for lack of Hope, rather than the job.

He pulled up to his brother's brick house in Broken Arrow and walked inside.

Mojo lay with his chin on Hope's T-shirt.

"I promised Tony I'd give it the summer," Grant told him. "But after that, let's head back to Colorado and that cool mountain air. I'll find a bomb squad gig in one of the bigger towns, or maybe I'll do training." He could work for the DEA or the Bureau of Alcohol, Tobacco, Firearms, and Explosives. "Or maybe search and rescue. You could be a hero again, without getting blown to hell."

Mojo whined, ears down.

"I miss her, too, buddy."

The dog's head lifted when Tony strode in. "Hey, Grant."

"Hey. What's up?"

Tony grimaced, rubbing his forehead. "I know I asked you to stay all summer, but I'd like to bring Jackie in, instead."

Grant blinked. Is that why his cousin was coming to visit? "Am I being fired?"

"No, no. Not fired. But she's really interested, and you're just humoring me."

"Yeah." Grant blew out a breath. "Sorry, man."

"Don't be."

"How much longer do you need me?"

"She can start Monday." Tony hesitated. "You got plans?"

"Nah." Grant shrugged. "But I really loved Colorado and might give it another whirl."

And try one more time to connect with Hope. He'd deal with Bear Creek. It wouldn't matter where it was, as long as he could be with her.

34
A Surprise Visit
-HOPE-

*H*ope booked an early morning flight to Tulsa to surprise Grant. She was glad his brother had been willing to give her the address. Had he kept his promise to keep her visit a secret?

She took a cab from the airport to the house, hoping to catch Grant before work, but no one was home.

So much for surprising him. Hope stood on the sidewalk and pulled out her phone to text.

A happy yelp was her only warning, before Baby charged her, dancing with joy, the leash swinging loose.

"Baby!" She flung her arms around him, eyes brimming. "I missed you!"

She laughed at the onslaught of licking, and the irony of Baby running away from Grant, but he didn't appear.

Instead, a young brunette rushed up the sidewalk. "Mojo! Bad dog!" She grabbed the leash. "I'm so sorry! He's usually such a good boy."

"He *is* a good boy." Hope knelt, rubbing his ears. "We go way back." She glanced curiously at the girl—a sister? A dog-sitter? A new girlfriend?

Have I waited too long? She swallowed. "My name's Hope."

"Hope?" The woman's face broke into a smile. "I'm Jackie, Grant's cousin. He's already at work. Come on in and you can wash off that dog drool." She opened the door and gestured inside. "He'll be home by six."

"Oh." Hope entered the house. Why had she assumed he'd have banker's hours?

The girl laughed at Hope's dismay. "Let me take you in to the office in Tulsa. They'll let him off early if you show up. Want something to drink while I change?"

"No, thanks. But I'd love to go to the office."

Baby rushed to bring Hope a ball. Instead of tossing it, she sat on the floor and invited him onto her lap for a hug. "I missed you so much."

AT A TALL GLASS office building downtown, Jackie and Hope took the elevator up to the suite labeled **Atkins,**

Calloway, and Rivera, Attorneys at Law, while she rehearsed her speech, palms damp.

"I'm Hope Hernandez, here to see Grant Calloway," she told the receptionist, a petite brunette with round oversize frames. "I don't have an appointment." Butterflies slam-danced in Hope's stomach and she held her breath.

The woman dialed the phone. "Mr. Calloway, Hope Hernandez is here to see you."

The loud, joyful, "Here? Now?" made the receptionist wince and pull the phone away, but happiness bubbled up inside Hope to hear it.

"I'll bring her right back." The woman stood, smiling. "This way."

Hope followed past offices with glass doors. Ahead, one burst open. A man in a gray suit entered the hallway, and she did a double-take.

"Grant?"

It was! Clean-shaven now, and breathtaking in a suit, crisp white shirt and navy tie paired with cowboy boots, but those same gorgeous eyes, crinkled with a wide smile.

It faded as he slowed. "Hope. Are you here for Mojo?"

"I stopped there first—" she began.

Grant winced.

Crap! Her entire speech went out the window. "But it was you that brought me here." She swallowed. "I came for you."

"For me?" Puzzlement transformed to joy, and Grant caught her in his arms, laughing. He spun her around and pulled her into an office. He crushed her to him. "It's great to see you," he whispered.

Hope closed her eyes and breathed in his scent, her head on his hard chest.

He pulled back and gazed down at her. "I've been thinking about what happened, and"—he took her hand and went on in a rush—"I was wrong to choose for you. I'm sorry."

"I'm sorry, too," Hope said. "That I got so angry. It was just the last straw, after Clay and Bear Creek Medical and Dad—I had no idea he'd interfered—and it hurt that you thought I was dishonest. I realized that you were probably right. I'd have let Clay off if he gave me a sob story."

She bit her lip. "It also made me wonder if I got the job only because Clay wasn't in the running, and that you thought so, too. I—"

"No. Oh, *hell*, no. There's no way he was as good as you. That's why he tried to run you off, because he couldn't compete."

His faith in her eased the tightness in her chest. "Part of it was feeling like I was failing Baby, too. And maybe you, since you were picking up so much of the slack for me. I was afraid you'd get tired of waiting for me."

"Oh, Pretty Girl. I'll wait as long as it takes, if you're willing to try joint custody again, and remember I'm on your side." Grant wrapped his arms around her.

Joy bloomed, clear and bright. "I'd love that," she said. "I'm in San Antonio now, signed up for locums work—temporary assignments with travel and less stressful hours—but I'm moving back to Colorado. I can visit, though."

"Really? I'm looking at jobs there."

She pulled away. "I thought you didn't like it."

"What? I loved Colorado. I didn't like *Bear Creek,* but I'd manage. I just want to be with you."

Oh, thank God. He hadn't lied to her. Relief swept away her last fear.

"I love you, Grant," she whispered.

"I love you, too, Pretty Girl."

She closed her eyes. Back where she belonged.

Grant' heartbeat beneath her cheek counted out the moments as he held her, strong and unhurried.

Sighing, Hope settled into his embrace, content to simply hold him, but the scent of his skin called to her, seductive. Imperative.

Breathless, she slid her hands up his chest.

Grant's arms loosened and he gazed down at her before he tilted up her chin and kissed her. Firm, gentle lips brushed hers and she wound her fingers into his hair, yearning.

He deepened the kiss, his tongue teasing and retreating, his thumb tracing her cheek. "Ah, Hope."

His husky voice gave her chills.

She trailed a finger down to his belt and tugged, craving him.

Grant kissed her throat and groaned, his breath coming short. "God, I missed you."

He murmured against her neck and nudged his leg between hers, pressing against the thin silk of her skirt, his hard thigh at the apex of hers.

Heat spread. She needed—

The doorknob rattled and a man strode in, saying, "Hey, Grant. Will you—Oh."

Grant pulled away with a suppressed oath, breathing hard, and cleared his throat. "Tony, this is Hope."

The guy, a stockier version of Grant but maybe five years older, smiled. "I guess you made it. Nice to meet you."

Grant glanced at him sharply.

Tony shook her hand and eyed his brother. "Take the rest of the day, before you set off the sprinkler system." He nodded to her and left.

"Damn." Grant blew out a breath. "I want you so bad, but I can't take you home since my cousin's staying with us. Let's get out of here before I strip you naked and push you up against the wall, glass door be damned." Bold brown eyes pinned her.

"Sounds great." She sagged, legs weakened with lust. "What do you have in mind?"

Grant's slow smile made her pulse flutter. "Give me a second and I'll get us a hotel with early check-in." He tapped into his phone with lean masculine hands. Tapped some more. He raised his eyebrows, stabbing at his cell, then frowned and dialed. "Hello, I'd like a room for tonight." His face went blank. "Okay, thanks."

He sat, pulling Hope into his lap.

He *was* glad to see her—that was no Kong in his pocket. She nuzzled his neck, anticipating, while he tried three other hotels.

"Seriously?" he asked the clerk. "Okay, thanks." He hung up and pressed the heel of his hand into his forehead. "She said most hotels are booked for a kids' karate tournament. Damn, damn."

He stared at her hungrily, until a slow smile curved his lips. "I know." He tapped at his phone again. "I'll book a place out of town later. Right now I'm feeling a sudden need for a car wash."

Hope blinked. *Oh, my.* "In broad daylight?" She

should feel scandalized, yet she was ready to drag him into the nearest utility closet.

Grant slid his hands down to her hips. "Tinted windows, suds everywhere. No one will walk in, past those spinning streamers. It's a perfect chance to get dirty *and* clean at the same time." He kissed her again, a naughty promise.

Her laugh was breathless. "How long would we have?"

"Only seven minutes, according to their site. But it'll take the edge off until tonight, when we can take all the time in the world." He nipped at her neck. "We'll have to compensate. Be ready to go."

"I'm ready now," she gasped when his thumb rubbed over her nipple.

His grin was wicked. "Every second matters. Let's trade: your panties for a condom." Grant slid his hand up her thigh beneath her skirt. "Don't worry," he whispered. "You still won't be naked." He hooked her panties and tugged them down.

She laughed and stepped out of them, arousal tingling.

He stuffed the red silk into his pocket and dug out a condom from his wallet. "It's all I have. Whatever you do, don't drop it."

Hope tucked it into her purse.

Grant put his arm around her and guided her toward the exit.

Air currents, stirred by the swish of silk, caressed her hidden bare flesh, and when she and Grant left the AC, the humidity made her melt.

In his pickup, Grant took off his suit jacket and tie, eyes dark with ardor. "Buckle in, Pretty Girl, and I'll take you for a ride."

He grinned, turned over the engine, and drove them to a three-bay automatic car wash. He stopped behind a gray Volvo, just entering the enclosure. The light above the bay turned red.

Grant set the timer on his watch. "We should have seven minutes to warm up while they go through. I guess it *is* a lucky number." He chuckled, leaning over to kiss her, while his hand traveled up her thigh.

Higher.

Currents of pleasure spread, from his mouth above to his fingers below and she arched her back, trembling.

"Grant, we won't need the car wash if you keep that up."

"Keeping it up isn't a problem, Pretty Girl." Grant placed her hand on his erection. "I just want to make sure you get a head start." His fingers resumed, deft and sure, stoking her need. He tangled his other hand in her hair and bent his head.

His lips roved her jawline, her neck. Stubble tickled, his breath feathering her skin before his mouth returned to hers.

Hope's orgasm tore through her.

"Hey, beautiful," he said, voice hoarse. Grant held her while she came down.

Taillights flared red in front of them, and the Volvo exited the bay. The green light came on.

"Thank God." Grant glanced at his watch. "A full seven minutes, too." He lowered the window, fed tokens into a panel, and pushed a button. He eased the pickup into the bay and set the parking brake. "You ready for me?"

Ready? She was *dying*.

"Yes," she breathed, ripping open the condom packet, and tensed to rise.

Grant vaulted to the passenger side. His gaze scorched her as he pushed the seat back and raised his hips. His belt creaked, the buckle clinking, and he shoved down his pants. His erection sprang free, a beaded drop at the tip. Grant's warm hands gripped her thighs beneath her skirt. He growled, "Put your other knee on the console, Pretty Girl, and hold on."

Water jetted onto the glass.

She positioned the condom and gripped his shoulders, hard beneath the thin, fine-woven dress shirt.

Outside, foam spattered the windows and the world dimmed.

"Let me just..." Grant nudged her open, fingers splayed over her hip.

She couldn't stand waiting. "Now." Hope sheathed him, gasping.

He groaned and dragged her hair to one side as he surged upward. Thrust again. And again. He pulled her shirt and bra strap off her shoulder. His gaze traveled from her breast to her eyes, and his tempo increased.

Outside, spinning streamers flogged the window, a rising crescendo beat to rival her pulse and the slap of Grant's bare thighs on her skin.

Grant's thumb moved, beneath her skirt, a slow circle that made her squirm. "Yeah?"

"Oh," she panted. "Grant, I'm almost—"

His hips bucked faster, driving her towards release, and she dissolved again with a little cry, clinging to his damp dress shirt. Grant's pelvis heaved again and he groaned, rocking into her, hands gripping her bottom.

Water spurted onto the glass, rinsing the foam away. The rivulets waned, leaving only the sound of heavy breathing.

The whoosh of drying jets surrounded them.

"Good timing," she panted. "Good all around, I'd say."

Grant kissed her, chuckling. "Tonight, I'll show you 'good,' Pretty Girl."

35
A Dream Find
- GRANT -

*I*t wasn't quite joint custody, but Hope lit up Grant's world when she visited on the weekends she wasn't on assignment.

In September, on Hope's last morning in Broken Arrow, he lay still, breathing in her green-apple scent, her head on his shoulder, and weighed his offers for K9 work in Colorado. Maybe he could join her there soon.

Hell, yeah. A couple and their dog, loose in the world. A pack.

Hope snuggled deeper into his chest and Grant reveled in her velvet skin.

She sighed. "I wish I didn't have to go."

"Me, too, Pretty Girl." Grant stroked her hip. "But I've got a surprise for you that might take the sting out."

She sat up, her long brown hair swinging. "You do? What kind of surprise?"

He grinned. "The kind that you find out about, instead of someone telling you." Grant laughed and scooted away from her playful swat. "Come on. I'll show you after breakfast. We have to bring Mojo, though."

"*Baby,* you mean." She eyed him, wheels turning. "How about breakfast to go, then?"

"Sounds great, as soon as I clean up."

Ignoring his nerves, Grant got cleaned up and dressed. He kissed Hope and took Mojo outside.

"*Let's go,* boy."

Mojo leaped into the bed of his truck, thrilled to go for a ride.

They picked up cinnamon rolls and coffee at a drive-through.

"So, the surprise is for him, too?"

"Yeah, I guess so. But mainly, he'll help you find it." Grant pulled into the little city park near Tony's silver Pathfinder. He scanned the grounds but didn't see his brother.

"Find it? It's hidden here?" Hope's eyes danced.

"Yep. Mojo doesn't know where, either. You'll have to work together. Go ahead and leash him up." He smiled at her expression: eagerness and exasperation mixed together.

While Hope got the dog, he texted Tony: **We're here.**

His brother replied, **Awesome. Been here 1 hr. U sure?**

Grant typed, **Never more certain.**

Tony responded, **Dumbass. I mean if they can't find it.**

Grant laughed. **Yeah... Mojo? Get outta here.**

Maybe he should have given Tony some direction, though. It'd be just like him to stash it next to a dumpster.

Hope approached with Mojo. "So, what's the surprise?"

He pulled an envelope out of the glove box and handed it to her, watching her face as she opened it and read the words he'd written:

You mean the world to me. Let Mojo help show you how much.

Hope frowned and looked up. "Now what?"

He grinned, hiding his nervousness. What if she thought it was stupid? "Ask him to help you find it." Grant had rubbed a dry bar of soap over the package and the card.

A smile spread across her face, and she crouched to proffer the card to Mojo. *"Find."*

He snuffled it and took off with an eager yelp,

wagging, as Hope trailed him on the long leash, laughing.

Nose low, he angled back and forth, methodical, from the benches at the front, across the grassy stretches, then he took off toward the rose arbor and pond, and Grant followed, trying to calm his nervous heart.

Mojo slowed, shoulder-deep in white camellia shrubs at the end of a bench, tail waving. He turned and sat, stock-still.

Grant couldn't breathe.

"What is it, Baby?" Hope peered into the foliage while Grant slipped Mojo a piece of jerky.

She squealed and dived, coming up with a little velvet box. Her hands shook as she opened it, and fire flashed from the solitaire within.

"Oh, my God," she whispered and looked up, eyes shining.

"We belong together. All three of us." Grant took the little box and knelt next to Mojo, and her eyes widened. "Marry me, Hope."

She flung herself into his embrace. "Yes," she said, her words muffled against his chest. "Oh, yes."

Hope thrust out her hand and Grant slid on the ring, then she turned to their dog.

"What a good boy. Know what this means, Baby?

No more joint custody —we'll be a real pack." She beamed at Grant, and he wrapped her in his arms.

He had everything he'd ever dreamed of, right here.

36
Colorado Roots

-HOPE-

*H*ope drove up the winding mountain road toward the little chalet, trying to suppress her excitement, while Grant rode shotgun. The diamond on her finger sparkled in the sunshine, and the aspens glowed with the first golden hints of fall.

Two months into looking at property near the ski resort town of Telluride, they'd not found the right place. This one had real promise: quick access to the highway for Grant's search and rescue work, though most of his time was taken up with training. Far enough for privacy and space, a gorgeous view, small enough to be cozy but big enough for a family some-day. The place backed up to national forest on one side, with access to trails and a creek. Their dog would love that.

"It's probably too good to be true," she said.

"I thought the same about you," Grant quipped.

"Anything's possible." He grinned, then switched to teasing Hope about her careful driving. "Aren't we trying to get there ahead of Joel, for a quick look around with no realtor? The way you baby your Jeep, I'm surprised you ever let it get off-road."

"We'll still beat him there. I thought you'd like to see the scenery." Hope waved at the snowy peaks that rose around them.

"I do like it." Grant tucked a strand of hair behind her ear. "Your profile's downright inspiring."

A long canine muzzle poked between them from the back.

"Hey, Mojo Baby," she said. "We're almost there."

Grant had put his foot down about calling their dog Baby. They'd settled on Mojo Baby Calloway Hernandez for his full name.

Hope rounded the last bend and slowed through a field of columbine interspersed with tall curly spikes of fireweed flower pods. In spring it'd be a carpet of blue and white—pink in the summer. Sunlight illuminated a steep-roofed Alpine chalet nestled at the foot of a huckleberry-covered slope, the cedar of the second-story balcony worn to a soft silver gray, and her heart skipped. "It's gorgeous." A place for a small garden. Room for kids and a dog.

Grant's gaze traveled over the property and

returned to rest on her, soft. "Beautiful," he agreed, a little smile tugging at his lips.

She pulled in and they hopped out next to the white **For Sale** sign.

Talk about a sign—Mojo Baby leaped out, raced around the little house, doubled back, and took up his Please Sit, at the base of the post. He grinned, tongue lolling and tail a blur.

She exchanged a glance with Grant.

He smiled and took her hand, pulling her close. "Looks like he approves."

An engine behind her ruined the moment, as the realtor drove up in a silver Mercedes and hopped out, the sun reflecting off his shiny pate.

"Morning," Joel called, smoothing his blue tie. "Saved the best for last, eh? Let's open 'er up."

Grant pointed to a spot on the porch. "Mojo Baby, *stay.*"

Joel retrieved the key from the lockbox and ushered them into the timber-frame structure, touting the charms of the place. "Hickory cabinets and granite countertops. The wood floor and mantelpiece were salvaged from a turn-of-the century sawmill. The fireplace stone is local. And look at that million-dollar view." He nodded at the huge windows overlooking the wildflower-dotted meadow in front.

Beyond, the huckleberry gave way to firs, then rugged rock crowned in snow-capped peaks.

I love it. Hope's hand tightened on Grant's.

They followed Joel upstairs. Two cozy bedrooms were tucked beneath the sloped ceiling, each airy and well-lit. The master bedroom boasted rustic furniture, a braided rug in front of a small glass-fronted woodstove, and a spacious bathroom. A small balcony faced the mountains and she stepped out into the fresh air.

"Look around and I'll see you outside." The realtor tramped downstairs.

"Nice and sturdy." Voice low, Grant pushed at the rail. Rock solid.

She imagined leaning on it, him behind her, his hands firm on her hips. It was enough to bring her to a simmer and she licked her lips.

"What do you think?" he asked. "Bring a quilt out here on a starry night..." Grant slid his arms around her and kissed her.

Hope melted inside. She pulled away, breathless. "I can see that. And this is beautiful." She grinned. "Might be risky with a place this nice, though—maybe I'll cut back on my AlphaMed work."

Grant laughed. "Oh, right. Like that'll ever happen. Let's put in an offer." He filled his lungs and called, "Mojo Baby, *come!*"

Hope smiled to see the dog race around the corner below.

He gave a short whuff and ran for the house.

"Are you going to ask his opinion, since we're a pack now?" she teased.

"Nah. He knows you're the alpha here."

37

Epilogue

*S*now swirled beyond the window of the little chalet as Hope crimped the crust on a chicken pot pie.

Mojo Baby watched from his cushion by the Christmas tree, ever-optimistic that she might relent and toss him a scrap.

She slid her creation into the oven and eyed the clock. Her locums work challenged her, but the short-term assignments allowed her to recover and to study for boards, enough to make her feel lucky, hearing her colleagues groan about finding the time.

She'd developed a real friendship with Joanna, who'd taken the position at Bear Creek Medical, and they got together whenever they could.

"How long will Grant be tonight, do you think?" Hope asked the dog. "It's a good sign that he hasn't come back for your help." If there were no lost hiker or avalanche victims, maybe he'd be home early.

She put another log on the crackling fire, brought in more wood, and fetched a bottle of wine from the cellar.

They'd settled into the perfect symbiosis: Grant held down the fort while she was away, and otherwise, she could spoil him with home-cooked meals and lots of attention.

Mojo Baby was happy, too, his Welcome Home Dance for Hope every bit as exuberant as the one he did for Grant.

The aroma of chicken and sage filled the house as Hope scrolled through listings to choose her next assignment, looking for a short job someplace warm and sunny, so Grant might be tempted to come along for a quick weekend break, though he was saving up vacation for their honeymoon in Fiji in late February.

"Tony will stay here after the wedding, so you won't have to go to a boarding kennel," she informed Mojo Baby, who grinned in appreciation, then leaped to his feet and rushed to the window.

He's home! Hope dusted off her hands, as giddy as the dog but more sedate, and crossed the room as Grant set his snowy boots in the tray near the door.

Mojo Baby pranced around him, wagging.

Grant hung up his coat and turned.

"Hey, Pretty Girl. It smells fantastic in here." Grant swept her up in a hug. "It's great to be home.

Hope smiled, squeezing him. "Thanks. I've got to make sure you keep coming back to me."

"Always." Grant bopped her nose and kissed her. "You're the best Find I've ever had."

The End

Did you enjoy *A Boy and his Dog*? Please leave a review—it makes a world of difference to an independent author who doesn't have "the machine" of a big publishing house at her back, and keeps Gus in puppy chow.

Check out the rest of the *All American Boy Series* (may be read in any order, as standalone books):

The Boyfriend Pact https://amzn.to/2Xy4Vjr
    Boy Business https://books2read.com/u/mgEyzz
    Boy I'm Yours My Book
    The Boy Upstairs https://bit.ly/TheBoyUpstairs
    Oh Boy! https://mybook.to/OhBoy
    Boyfriend Material https://tinyurl.com/yzknry6j
    The Boyfriend Checklist
    The Boy I Shouldn't Want
    The Boy I Can't Forget

The Boy Under the Gazebo https://geni.us/TheBoyUndertheGazebo

The Boy I Loved https://www.books2read.com/theboyiloved

Inked Boy

Boy and the Family Plan https://tinyurl.com/yzkawvel

Small Town Boy http://mybook.to/SmallTownBoy

Want more Holiday escapes? *A Boy and his Dog* is the *first* novel in Chloe Holiday's new **AlphaMed Series™** which features medical and/or military romances, each a standalone story with no cliffhangers. Check out Chloe's website for cool snippets and news about the next story and to subscribe to her newsletter!

Crave more romance in the meantime? Each novel in *The Helios Series* is a stand-alone story with a Happily Ever After—NO cliffhangers!

Enemies-to-lovers, workplace romance, military men and women, medical subplots, thriller elements, love triangles, adventure ... there's something for everyone, and some are available in audiobook formats. Check them out on Amazon and read on for a sample of *Finders, Keepers!*

FINDERS, KEEPERS SAMPLE

Finders, Keepers
By Chloe Holiday
Copyright 2020

♥ CHAPTER 1: INTO THE NIGHT ♥

Just three more hours to go. Softly humming Frosty the Snowman to herself, Farrah made the rounds with her mail cart, already excited about Global Marketing's party tonight. Or rather, Justin's reaction to her killer new dress.

Farrah stepped into the copy editor's cubicle, her short red skirt trimmed with white marabou feathers swinging. She dropped a couple of manila envelopes onto his desk and resumed her circuit through the quiet maze of workstations.

The cart took a sudden lurch to the left—the darned wheel stuck *again*. The detour triggered the motion-activated Rudolph on the new guy's desk —and the glares of coworkers—as a tinny version of *Grandma Got Run Over by a Reindeer* blared.

The new guy smiled, his eyes on her short skirt.

Maybe not her best choice—he probably thought she did it on purpose, just to meet him. Farrah rotated the offending wheel and shuddered: a gummy chunk of red candied fruit clung to the rubber. *Who really eats fruitcake?*

The guy turned from his computer. "Hey. I'm Brad. Need a hand?"

She smiled at his eagerness. "Can I get a tissue?"

"Absolutely." He yanked two out of a box and handed them to her, grinning.

"Thanks. I'm Farrah. Nice decorations—I love the holidays." She extracted the nasty wad of gunk from the wheel.

"Will you be at the party tonight?" he asked.

"Yes, with my boyfriend, Justin." Farrah pretended not to notice the way his face fell. "Nice to meet you, Brad." She tossed the crumpled tissue in his trash bin.

It would take more than fruitcake to dent her

mood, her usual holiday cheer sparked higher by anticipation. Still humming, she finished her rounds and wrestled the mail cart back into place. Her stomach growled at the smell of cinnamon from the plug-in air freshener. *It's a break from Pumpkin Spice, anyway.*

A few festive cubicles were decorated in bright tinsel garlands or Hanukkah dreidels, but this year most employees had refrained after Shelby, the new department manager, made known her distaste for such "vulgarity."

Someday I'll be free of Shelby and the corporate world, too.

At least the witch hadn't extended her disapproval to attire yet. In addition to her red skirt, Farrah wore small holly earrings and her pine-green nails glittered with tiny candy cane decals. Her late grandmother always told her, *"Have fun while you're young, honey—it gets beat out of you soon enough."* Farrah had taken those words to heart.

No one was going to ruin her holidays, not even her dragon lady boss. Tonight's party was destined to be wonderful. She smiled, imagining the look on Justin's face when he saw her in that glamorous new dress, and slipped back to her cubicle. Her "in" box brimmed with more documents to photocopy. One eye on the clock, Farrah raced through her drudge work.

The moment five o' clock arrived, she hurried to gather her bag and coat, humming *Rudolph the Red-Nosed Reindeer.*

She ran into her friend Nicole in the hallway.

"You're still coming tonight, right?" Nicole asked. "Ryan texted he can't make it." She sighed, tucking strands of long brown hair behind her ear. "I hate office parties."

"Oh, no. I'm sorry he can't come." *Poor Nicole.* What a bummer. "Don't worry, I'll be there. It'll be fun—free food, dancing, and an open bar. We can hang out, since Justin will be off schmoozing." Farrah slid her arms into her puffy orange coat. "Justin's so psyched his photographs are on display at the gallery, during Global's party. Maybe someone with deep pockets will notice."

She smiled, thrilled to have played a small role in his success. "I even sprang for a new dress—it's the only way he'll pay attention to me at all." She pulled on her knit cap, a kaleidoscope of orange, blue, red, and green, the matching mittens in one hand.

"That hat's great." Nicole grinned, her eyes on the floppy tassel. "And the mittens are perfect for you."

"Thanks. They're the last things my grandma made for me. She used all my favorite colors. Said the tassel would bounce just like me." A lump rose in her throat and she looked down as she dug through her bag. "I made you something."

She presented Nicole with a small package wrapped in stamped brown paper, bound with a curled red ribbon, a sprig of rosemary tucked under it. "Merry Christmas."

"Thanks. I'll bring yours on Monday." Nicole hesitated. "Shall I open it now?" At Farrah's nod, she pulled off the ribbon and unfolded the paper, revealing little white cubes of handmade soap, bits of red petals showing beneath the surface. She lifted one square and inhaled. "Ooh, is this your latest batch? It smells wonderful. What is it, apple?"

"Scented geranium. Glad you like them. I've gotta go—see you later." Farrah pulled on her mittens.

Her step buoyant from Nicole's reaction to her gift, Farrah left the building's warmth for the chilly streets of Washington, D.C. Head down, she leaned into the biting wind on her way to the Metro. She had to tug off her mitten to fish out her card. The clumsiness and temporarily cold fingers were no reason to switch to gloves. *These are warmer, anyway,* her grandma had said, and she was right. Farrah felt warm through and through every time she wore them.

Farrah arrived at her tiny apartment near the Convention Center two hours before the party. She'd have time to redo her nails to something sophisticated before Justin arrived to pick her up.

It was no trouble to tone down her look, since it was such an important night to him. She smoothed her spiky blonde hair, washed her face, applied understated makeup, and slipped on elegant dangly earrings that would appeal to Justin.

A spritz of perfume, and then excitement bubbled when she pulled out that dress: a slinky sheath of red with a halter neck that flared into a mermaid skirt. Just zipping it up made her feel sexy and daring. Confident.

She slid her feet into strappy red heels and spun in front of the bedroom mirror—not much twirl in the skirt, but it did look good. Her heart kicked up a notch. Justin would be here any minute.

Her apartment door banged open. "Hey, it's me," he called, followed by the thump of his laptop case and the soft clink of his coat buttons on the hard wooden chair. His voice came nearer. "You should have seen the traffic—"

Farrah sashayed out of the bedroom.

He stopped mid-sentence, lean and handsome in a dark suit and tie. His dark bangs cascaded artfully over one eye, his shoulder-length hair sleeked back into a ponytail. "Whoa."

She grinned, thrilled by his approval, still not quite believing that in this cutthroat town of social climbers and ambitious professionals, this sophisticated artist had chosen her.

His eyes traveled from her breasts to her feet and back to her face. "Damn, that's a sexy look." He took two steps forward and slid his arms around her. "I don't suppose we have time to do anything before we go?"

"On your big night? Not on your life." He'd have one eye on the clock.

Justin laughed. "You're right. I don't want to be late. Maybe later I can get some action." He grinned, caught her hand, and rubbed his thumb suggestively between her fingers. "Nice, with the plain red nails. That kiddie stuff is fun, but this is the smart choice for an important event."

She blinked, but he didn't mean anything by it.

He's just nervous. Farrah hugged him. "Don't worry, you'll do fine."

He let her go. "Let's head over. If we go now, we can just eat the hors d' oeuvres and skip dinner."

"Ha, ha." She rolled her eyes. "I thought we were going out first." Farrah was the one struggling with money, but he had the starving artist vibe down pat: Brooding, dark, handsome, cynical.

"I know, but do you mind? I'm just so psyched, I want to get there early."

"Okay." Farrah understood his eagerness. A brilliant photographer, favoring stark black and white portraits with a sensual edge. Maybe tonight would be the big break he'd waited for.

She worried she'd lobbied too hard for Global to have their party at the gallery, but if the corporate art director liked Justin's work, that could be a huge opportunity for him to connect with companies all over the world. She scooped up her purse, shrugged into her coat, and picked up her hat and mittens.

"You're wearing those? With that dress?" Justin wrinkled his nose. "I guess you can check your coat, but can't you leave those in the car?"

She crossed her arms and raised her eyebrows.

He held up his hands defensively, his smile placating. "I know you love the wild colors, but orange and blue clash with your red dress, and you look so beautiful tonight."

"Love me, love my hat." Farrah sniffed. So what if the colors clashed for forty seconds? It was no big deal to pull a hat on and off her short hairstyle.

"Besides, once they see your photos, people are going to be looking at you, not me." She stuck her mitten through the crook of his elbow. "Let's go."

Outside the art gallery, Farrah pulled off her hat and mittens, rolled them tightly, and stuffed them into her clutch. Easy enough to do that, if it helped with his nervousness. Chamber music played in the background as they entered, Justin's biceps tense under her fingertips. "Don't worry. You'll do great," she whispered.

His arm stayed rigid beneath her hand. Maybe the classical strains would mellow him.

Farrah's quick glance confirmed he'd kept his promise: the photographs were unidentifiable. She relaxed, looking forward to the driving tempo of dance music after the address from Global's president.

She introduced Justin to her boss, Greg, while the new manager Shelby looked on with her usual faint sneer. "This is my boyfriend, Justin, the one I told you about. The photographs on the walls are his."

"Oh? I was just about to take a closer look at them." Greg smiled at Justin. "Why don't you get something to eat and then give me a tour? I can see if anyone else wants to tag along, too."

"Sure, that would be great." Justin's smile looked relaxed, but instead of heading to the food, he betrayed his nerves by launching into a rapid barrage of chatter about his inspiration and influences.

After a few minutes, Greg said, "We'd better get something to eat before the president starts his address."

Justin flashed her a smirk as Greg and Shelby strolled toward the buffet, but Farrah worried they'd only said it as an excuse.

"I think it's going well," Justin whispered. "Let's get some chow."

Farrah snickered—though he might diss her fashion choices, he wasn't above the occasional earthiness that clashed with his elegant facade. She watched the revelers but didn't see Nicole.

Farrah had to admit that Global put out a nice spread. Shrimp and fancy crackers, cheese balls, bacon-wrapped scallops, crudites with dip—there were things so exotic they needed labels. "Pomegranate Chevre Crostini," she read. "Too bad my bag is stuffed full—I can't smuggle any of this home."

Justin shot her a look.

Did he think she was serious? Farrah pushed

down irritation—he got so uptight sometimes with big projects.

She glanced up at the black-and-white photos of shadowed nudes, with a little thrill that Justin saw her that way. Sensuous and tasteful. Serious. Just like Justin. If only he could relax a bit and have some fun. "They do have an open bar." Maybe a glass of wine would help his nerves.

They moved down the table, and she was careful not to overfill her little plate despite the black hole in her stomach. On their first date three months ago, he'd looked askance at her loaded plate when they'd gone to a buffet—she'd skipped lunch that day so she could afford to go out for dinner—and ever since she'd been certain to never again take so much, instead going back for seconds. But never thirds.

They stood at the back, nibbling cheese puffs as the president's speech wound down.

"Oh, this pomegranate thing is really good," she whispered. "Try one."

"Mm, hmm." Justin scanned the crowd. Naturally, he'd be looking for people he wanted to chat up, now that the speech was over.

A woman with a sleek dark chignon nodded at him and swept past. His gaze followed her.

Farrah frowned at him.

"That's someone I spoke with about modeling for

me. Her name's Annika." He smiled down at Farrah. "I might need to talk shop with her some."

"Sure." Farrah bit off half a shrimp. Of course, Justin had to make the most of this opportunity, and the fact that he'd taken pains to show her it was professional helped assuage any jealous feelings. Besides, she'd have Nicole to chat with soon. "You've got to take advantage of your time here." She nodded toward Greg, who shook hands with the president, then headed toward them.

Justin set down his plate, squared his shoulders, and faced her. "Do I have anything in my teeth?"

"You look fine." Farrah watched Justin, outwardly confident, walk up to Greg and the new manager. Shelby stepped close to Justin, but maybe she had to because of the music's loud, pulsing techno beat. Farrah's eyes narrowed as the shrew put her hand on his forearm, laughing.

"Farrah! Oh, my God, you look wonderful." Nicole, wearing a modest black sheath, grabbed her in a quick hug and stepped back again. "Let's see that dress."

Farrah grinned and twirled. "I'll be paying it off for months, but maybe it'll be worth it." It would be, if Justin was ready to take their relationship to the next level if it went well tonight. He'd hinted about her moving in with him once, and her lease was coming up soon, but he'd been so distracted since the photography symposium in Europe. "Justin likes it."

Nicole huffed. "Only a dead man would ignore that dress. Look around. All those eyes aren't hungry for the buffet."

Farrah glanced around the room. It was true that the single men—even some of the married ones—gave her appreciative smiles, maybe more than she got with her usual Bohemian look. "Yeah, right. Those guys are into anything with a pulse."

Nicole laughed. "Are you crazy? You're sizzling hot." She peered at the people talking at the bar, then at the dancers. "Justin's tied up promoting, I guess? You're still going to dance, right?"

"Heck, yeah, I am. I can't waste this dress just because my boyfriend's off doing business. Let's go." She took hold of Nicole's arm. "You, too, girl—you can still have fun even if your man is absent. Come on."

They stopped at the edge of the dance floor. An eclectic mix of couples moved to a compelling beat: trim young bodies with hip-hop moves, and portly management types—some stiff and restrained, and others already lubricated, hamming it up.

"Ladies? Care to dance?" A tall man with tousled, dirty blond hair stopped in front of them, a shorter dark-haired guy in his wake. New, or contractors?

The blond spun Farrah onto the floor as the other man pulled Nicole, protesting feebly, into the fray. Farrah lost herself in the rhythm, the warmth and energy of the crowd invigorating.

"I'm going to get a drink—you want one?" Her current partner bent to talk over the music.

"No, thanks. I need to find my boyfriend. It was fun dancing with you." And it had been fun, exactly what she needed. But she had to remember she was here mainly for Justin. A flash of guilt flickered through her. Time to go find him, in case he needed her support. He'd been so nervous about tonight —that was the reason he'd picked at her.

She grabbed a glass of wine and weaved through the crowd. Where was he? Had it gone poorly, and he'd sought time alone? Heart sinking, Farrah stopped outside the men's room as a middle-aged man came out. "Excuse me, I'm looking for my boyfriend. Is anyone else in there?"

He shook his head and ambled back to the crowd.

She circled the edge of the dance floor again and ran into Nicole. "Have you seen Justin?"

Nicole frowned. "No. The men's room, maybe?"

"Nope. I just checked. I'll keep looking." She smiled at Nicole and set her empty glass down on a linen-draped table near the bar. *Justin knows this place. Did he need a breather?*

She dug her phone out of her overstuffed clutch and tapped out a message.

Farrah: Where are you?

No response.

Her brow furrowed. Maybe he'd gone to the offices or other rooms? She checked her phone again, then shoved it back into the wadded knitwear in her bag. His hopes were so high—had someone said something to crush them? Worry edged in; he could be so sensitive. Underneath his facade, Justin was vulnerable—it was one of the things that drew her to him. He probably needed her now.

She walked along the art gallery's back wall to a door marked "Private" and slipped through into a long corridor. Had he ducked into one of the rooms? The offices were marked "Vice President" and "Human Resources."

Farrah bit her lip—how much trouble would she get in if she were caught here? She reached out to the first knob and hesitated. She grasped the handle—locked. No alarms shrilled, no guards came running. Farrah breathed out a soft laugh of relief and tried the next knob. Nothing.

A thin slit of light revealed the third office door was open just a crack. She put her hand on the knob and paused. If he was devastated, he might not want to be disturbed. She held her breath and pushed the door gently open to peek in...

What happens next? Get **Finders, Keepers** to find out! It's also available in audiobook format at your favorite distributor.

ACKNOWLEDGMENTS

If it weren't for the small but mighty army at my back, this book would never have happened: my marvelous critique partners from Scribophile, my fantastic beta readers, those fans who wrote to me, detailing how much they enjoyed my previous books, the inspiration from members of the Writers' Coop of the Pacific Northwest, and lastly, my fabulous, patient spouse.

I appreciate you all!

ABOUT THE AUTHOR

Chloe writes steamy, fun stories about ordinary people in extraordinary circumstances, smart women and men who aren't jerks. About friendships, either close women or a good bromance. She wants all the feels: the thrill of a smoldering gaze or the barest brush of fingertips, the shocked gasp at the under-handed villain, the angst of heartbreak, the joy of reunion, and of course, happily ever after!

She hates to read the same old thing, with only the names and places changed, so her goal is to bring you a fresh, fun, NEW story every time, with NO CLIFFHANGERS!

More than anything, she wants to create a rollick-ing, great story that readers can't put down, one where love prevails in the end, one that will whisk them away from their own tribulations.

Come join her at http://www.chloeholiday.com/

instagram.com/chloeholiday27

Made in the USA
Monee, IL
08 March 2022